Praise for A.

Small Forgotten Moments

"A spellbinding, intoxicating journey into the dark heart of obsession. … another beautiful, heart-wrenching, epic masterpiece. I loved it."
Tom Gillespie, author of The Strange Book of Jacob Boyce

"A soulful tale of painting, secrets and longing, which draws the reader into a world of mystery and memory - an enchanting read."
Leonora Meriel, author of The Unity Game

"It's beguiling, haunting, beautifully paced and it kept me hooked to the very end."
Michael Walters, author of The Complex

Grace & Serenity

"The gripping story of a girl´s downward spiral to the bottom. A FINALIST and highly recommended!"
The Wishing Shelf Book Awards

"The story of a desperate young woman who finds herself on a difficult path, and hurtles towards a thrilling conclusion. A tense and compelling read."
- Vikki Patis, author of In the Dark

You. I. Us.

"It's expert storytelling and skilful writing when so much is expressed in so few words…"
- Cathy Ryan, Between the Lines

"These honest stories are deeper and more expansive than the words on the page."
- Ann S. Epstein, author of The Great Stork Derby

That Sadie Thing

and other stories

Also by Annalisa Crawford

Cat & The Dreamer

Our Beautiful Child

You. I. Us.

Grace & Serenity

Small Forgotten Moments

That Sadie Thing

and other stories

Annalisa Crawford

Published 2022
First edition published 2013, Second (ebook) edition 2021
Third edition (paperback) 2022

Cover Photo by Charlota Blunarova on Unsplash

To my husband Peter, forever

Contents

That Sadie Thing   11

Irish Green   19

Beth   24

The Walking Dead   30

Open Windows   37

Omelette   42

Shadows of Autumn   51

Portrait of the Painter   60

The Girl who is Good   67

Tasting the Grass   75

Knickers and Wellies   79

The Guitar at the Centre of the World   83

My Mother's Mother's Mother   89

Rain Dancing   95

Story Credits   105

Acknowledgements   107

That Sadie Thing

Take Sadie: there was nothing special about Sadie. Just an ordinary woman stood at an ordinary bus stop. Attractive, but then most women are; they just don't know how to make the best of what they have. They layer on far too much make-up, or don't wear enough; they wedge voluptuous thighs into unyielding mini-skirts or conceal slim figures beneath swathes of heavy fabric; they dye their hair an assortment of shades when the natural colour is unrivalled. Mostly they try too hard; and they fail.

There was nothing special about Sadie; except that I met her.

I can picture her now. She wore a black trouser suit and carried a briefcase; and yet her handbag was the shape of a flower, red and yellow, slung diagonally across her chest. Her watch, peeking out from the cuff of the sombre jacket, was a cheap silver thing, with a pink face and no numbers. These things intrigued me, these little touches of individuality nudging out from her corporate façade.

But that wasn't the reason I met her. It was just an ordinary day, at an ordinary bus stop, with rain threatening and the buses running late again. I didn't know it was her at first, of course; I didn't even know her name until that day. I never normally know their names, because women don't normally introduce themselves to the heavy breather on the end of the line.

Anyway, Sadie…

"It happened again last night," she said before she had a name, not bothering to lower her voice.

"Another call?" her companion asked.

I tuned in straight away; there was something pitiful in her tone, and I needed to know more. She was stood behind me in the queue, so I twisted a little hoping to snatch a glance of this intriguing woman.

"Have you reported it yet?"

"The phone company told me go to the police."

I held my breath. Could it be possible? Was this really her? I turned further, hoping to disguise the movement as a quest for my bus; but I looked straight at her by mistake. She stared back, and we were caught like that for several moments. Her eyes were a lovely blue, like the colour of a Bounty wrapper, narrowing with a brief flicker of consternation. I smiled weakly and made sure I broke the connection first.

"Have you done it?"

"Done what?" she asked distractedly.

Several times I felt her move behind me. Did she recognise me? A stupid thought, of course not—she'd only ever heard me breathe. Besides, I'm not the type of person you remember. Even if I stood at this bus stop, right in front of her every morning for a whole year, she wouldn't recognise me. But why am I giving you hints? This isn't my story.

Her friend sighed. "Phoned the police?"

"Oh, um… no, not yet."

"Sadie!"

Sadie. That name. From her appearance that day I thought she was a lawyer or executive, someone who made fast-paced decisions or negotiated multi-million-pound deals. But Sadie is the name of a… a dancer, or maybe a cellist. Yes, *Sadie* should be a cellist, her ball-gowned thighs straddling its broad frame, tanned arms cradling the sleek polished neck, her head swaying back and forth in time with a rousing aria. Sadie should sleep all day and practise all night in a vast loft apartment where the acoustics give perfect resonance; she should walk bare footed on the wooden floors.

She shouldn't spend her days behind a desk telling other people how to do their jobs; it was a shame such a wonderful name was being wasted.

"I haven't had the time," said Sadie in defence, and scooped in a large breath. "Anyway, I thought it would stop. I mean, how bored do you have to be to sit at home and phone people like that?"

Her friend hesitated before replying, leaning in. "You do realise that pervert is probably wanking off, don't you?" Her voice was the merest of whispers; I barely heard it, and the man in front of me didn't hear it at all because he didn't react. You'd think he'd react to the word *wank* at eight o'clock in the morning, wouldn't you?

"Uh?"

"He probably works himself up into a frenzy just thinking about calling you, and… when you answer…"—I imagined one eyebrow raised, prompting—"the sound of your voice…" she pushed on, awkwardly. "You know…"

I saw her hands move explosively in my peripheral vision. Several people turned in unison, and Sadie's friend flushed as she realised her voice had risen.

Sadie looked concerned, then she smiled. "Well, then, I hope I'm helping." They were past the point of having a private conversation. Sadie knew the entire queue was listening, so she was performing. There were one or two smiles, one or two scowls of disapproval. I seethed. I longed to intervene and say *actually, no, it's not like that at all.*

But the number eleven arrived, and I was left alone and seething.

The thing about Sadie, the thing which compelled me to dial her number almost to the exclusion of all others, was she didn't scream.

Nuisance phone calls are a long-term investment.

The first of anything is always disappointing, yet we never learn: the first day of a coveted job; the first bite of chocolate cake after a week-long detox; the first night out in your impossibly high, killer-red stilettoes. Your frenzied anticipation diminishes to barely more than faint pleasure when you realise that the shoes blister your heels until it's impossible to walk and the chocolate cake is a bit dry and has a strange waxy aftertaste.

The first phone call is always disappointing, because the person on the other end takes no notice.

Picture it: the phone rings while you're cooking dinner. You remove the boiling pan from the heat and answer. "Hello?" You wait. "Hello? Anybody there?"

If you're a patient person you might repeat yourself a couple of times; if not, you'll hang up straight away. Nevertheless, you'll shrug and think nothing more of it.

The second, third, fourth time will be the same. I'll catch you just as you're leaving for an aerobics class or night out with friends. I'll call just as you're stepping into a candle-lit, lavender-scented bath. Not on purpose: I am not a stalker. I don't plan these calls for these times; I don't wish your anger. My timing will simply be bad, and you might even ignore me.

But what about the tenth time, the twentieth? What would you do then?

Picture it *now*.

You're sitting on the sofa with a good book after an exhausting day at work. You became a little twitchy earlier as you turned the corner into your road, but you paused at the front door, key in hand, until you felt calmer. You paused again after you opened the door, relieved the phone wasn't already ringing. You wriggled your toes out of your shoes; you peeled off your one-size-too-small skirt and tights, and swapped them for soft brushed-cotton pyjamas.

Now you're curled up with the novel, a glass of wine nestled in your lap, and for the first time all day you feel yourself fully unwind, sinking into a fluffy pink cushion—not a frown nor a smile, not a single thought beyond the chicken casserole simmering in the oven and the words of the book twirling on the page. You feel every bit of tension receding, and you hope today will be the first day in weeks when you don't get one of *those* calls.

Too late. I'm already dialling.

You jump. You taste the fear; swallow the terror. You don't want to answer. And you hesitate. But what if it's your mother phoning to tell you that Aunt Lily has been taken into hospital? What if it's your best friend Clare phoning to ask whether you'd consider being her bridesmaid next summer?

You clamber reluctantly from your ball and shuffle towards the phone. It seems like a million steps away as you listen to every ring, hoping each one will be the last and you'll be saved from answering. But the ringing goes on and on and on and on…

"Hello?"

Nothing.

Not a sound.

"Hello?" you say again, a little louder in case your mother (because it *is* your mother, isn't it?) was distracted and didn't hear you.

Your voice isn't as commanding as it was at the beginning. You're being eroded, your whole self is being chipped away, and a new self, a new identity is forming in its void.

And, anyway, it's not really your mother on the end of the line, is it?

"Who is this?" you'll say, attempting dominance, but you know you're being ineffective. "Answer me, you fucking moron!"

You slam the receiver down, hover your hand over the phone, pick it up and dial 1471 even though you know I've concealed my number from you. You're shaking. You stare at your hands and at the phone and consider unplugging it. But why should you? Why should you feel scared in your own home? In defiance, you leave it plugged in.

You pace up and down, just for the sake of doing *something*, aimless and anxious. You look at the clock, look at your watch. Maybe you jump up and down or hit the wall with your fist. That's what I'd do; my first reaction would be violence. But, as I'm not there, you have to hit something else. Your stride eases until you're standing frozen in the hall and confronting the phone.

Nothing happens.

Will I call back? Twice in one night—have I ever done that?

You don't know, you can't remember; because there's no before or after, no fixed point to which you can attach anything. There's just me, and a phone which has become the enemy.

Finally, you'll sit back down, not on the sofa, not with the book. You'll sit stiff and scared in the antiquated armchair with the tall back and hard seat, the one that Aunt Lily gave you when she went into the home. You'll fetch the bottle of wine and top up your glass. You're not at ease; your hand twitches. You'll watch the clock until your flatmate comes home, and then you'll be bright and jovial; and when she asks what's wrong, you'll smile and say, "Nothing."

Mostly, they scream; or blow a whistle; or shout, *what do you want from me?* like a clichéd 1950s horror film. And when I know they've finally noticed me, that they're taking me seriously, I stop. It's the panic I need, leeching it from them, filling myself up. I don't want to hurt them; I just want to be a part of them for a while.

But the thing about Sadie was she didn't scream. What I thought she must have done was put the phone down on the table and walked away, so that while I was listening, waiting for her to crack, she was in a different room ignoring me.

It was only when she was stood behind me at the bus stop that I realised I was affecting her. It was gratifying. She was agitated which made her normal, rather than the cold-blooded bitch I was starting to imagine. But she wasn't screaming; and that was curious. If she wasn't going to play by the rules, how did she think I'd ever leave her alone?

I think *you* would shout. *Speak to me… Say something!* Yes, just like that. You would demand, you would want to be in control. But that would ruin everything. Because then you'd see me for who I really am. My voice would give me away, and you'd laugh out loud with bemused relief. I don't know: would it be a relief if you knew I was a woman too?

A woman is safe, friendly, comforting. You run to a woman for help. A woman can't harm you the way you fear. A woman will hug you and steer you from peril the way you'd offer the same to someone in need. Wouldn't she?

It will be during the night when you finally break down. It almost always is. Because the darkness claws us back to irrational childhood fears. You actually believe the person on the end of the phone is the Bogeyman calling from the depths of your wardrobe. Then you wake properly, and the suffocating darkness makes you precarious and terrified. So, you don't want to answer the shrill ring, but you're an adult and you have a responsibility to.

That stabbing silence is so familiar to you now. It chills you.

And you scream; a blend of panic and fury and exhaustion, until you have no energy left.

Your vulnerability and fear are so pure: the perfect scream. And you do it so well. You won't receive another call from me because I'll be searching for new numbers, new women.

In the days to come you'll notice something missing, but you won't be quite sure what. When you realise it's only me, you'll shake yourself into a smile and be liberated. You might think about that scream and wonder where the strength came from; but it's over, and you don't want to reflect too hard in case you wish me back again.

To be accurate, I'm providing a service. You should be thanking me. I've given you an unparalleled opportunity to understand who you truly are. You'll know something pure about yourself that no one else could even contemplate when they stand next to you in a queue or sit beside you on a train. A saturated scream, uninhibited and unreasoned, is a release.

Everyone should scream.

The thing about Sadie was she didn't scream.

She stopped answering her phone.

My calls increased.

The silence unnerved me.

I stood at the bus stop waiting for a glimpse—an endless stream of commuters pouring from each vehicle. But never her. After that first time, I didn't see her again.

She became all-consuming, to the point I where was phoning her constantly, until I knew her number from memory. And yet she still didn't answer.

I stayed awake, night after night, dialling and redialling.

Later, the number became unobtainable; and I was left without that satisfying feeling of finality.

Three weeks ago, I read about an inquest into the suicide of Sadie Merson, driven to the point of unqualified delirium by a series, over eighteen months, of silent phone calls.

If only Sadie had screamed.

Irish Green

I paint my toenails green: Irish Shamrock green. I shiver by the gaping French window as the eager March sun vanishes behind a rogue snow cloud, a piercing winter breeze taking its place. Once the Irish Shamrock is dry, I swaddle my feet in thick woollen socks, hiding the colour away, and warm them by the radiator.

My toes are camouflaged as I walk barefoot. I carry my shoes, swinging them beside me, and dance through the dew-damp grass to an early morning lecture. My ankles are embellished with three delicate gold chains and a small Celtic cross tattooed just above the bone. My pale, freshly-shaved legs are shrouded in drifting Indian silks printed with patterns of the ocean. By the time I reach the grey stone building at the end of a long stretch of prefabricated huts, the sun is strong enough for me to remove my cardigan and feel the soft breeze on my arms.

People call me Pixie. Either *The* Pixie, or simply *Pixie*, as though this is my name; and truly, I've almost forgotten my name, it's been so long since anyone has used it.

These people who do not know my name stare after me as I walk by in the late afternoon heat, my clothes slick with a salty glow. The drooping lawn is covered with layers of supine students showering in the lingering sun after a hard day in the library or lecture theatre. Pens, books, laptops scattered next to them, ignored; there's a low hum of voices, but no one is really talking. It's too hot to talk or to listen; too hot to eat or study.

I spend the shimmering sultry evenings alone, gazing from my window as people head in clusters towards the student bar, hand-in-hand pairs or large rowdy groups. I feel an urge to follow them, to sit in a dark corner and be part of them. I change my clothes and slip in unnoticed, downing bottles of beer with foreign names and pretending I belong.

Later, as I leave through the throng of dancers, a hand brushes my waist, then grasps as though to pull me back inside. I don't see whose hand, and I'm dragged in the opposite direction by the swell of drinkers at the bar.

The night-time loses potency with this sudden shift outside. The silent and empty campus, calm and cold. I wrap my arms around my body for a little extra warmth; the chill catches out the t-shirt wearers who are pursuing the last allusion of summer. Stars glint through the glassy sky; the smell of a real fire lingers on the air.

Back in my room I make hot chocolate and wear a thicker t-shirt to bed. The curtains are open when I wake; rain hangs in the sombre morning mist. Soon, I'll be compelled into heavy brown boots to protect my feet from puddles settling along the kerb. I'll no longer paint my toenails because they won't be seen.

"Hey Pixie!"

I flinch at the mockery in his voice and refuse to react. I stare instead at the path ahead and fight my blushes. If I did turn there'd be a group of Freshers ready to laugh at my optimism, or third year Economics girls who'd eye me—from their belligerent cliques—with a mixture of envy and resentment.

People, the people who do not know my name, gossip about me in corridors, their voices hushed like the purr of wind between branches; their eyes darting in case I'm just around the next corner listening to them. And when I have no choice but to pass by, they laugh at these private jokes—with extravagant giggles—as though I care what they think of me. I've heard them only because they want me to hear them.

Those are the rules we observe, a tacit understanding that one of us will always be superior. In truly secret moments they hide from me, as though this is a war.

"Hey, Pixie," comes the call again, louder this time, softer. Closer, breathless.

I slow my pace, curious; a vague longing that this time it'll be different, that this time the voice calling my name will be different. And my heart sinks at my own gullibility.

Footsteps run behind me and stop. "Hey Pixie," he says softly.

So, this time I turn.

It's growing dark and the path is deserted; lights from the library building cast an orange glow across his face. He smiles. I wonder what I look like with my nose red and my ears numb. His dark hair, brown or possibly black, tangles across his illuminated face and he pushes it from his eyes with a hand wrapped in the sleeve of his outsized jumper. My own hands tingle through thick woollen gloves.

"I don't talk to strangers." My breath hangs between us in the frozen air.

"We don't have to be strangers." He puts his hand on my waist and it feels familiar.

Two black-cloaked Halloween witches run past us, wailing and cackling on their way to a party. We feign fright and laugh at each other. I watch, long after the witches have merged with the dark shadows of large oak trees. I wonder briefly what it would be like to be someone else, someone who isn't mocked and ridiculed.

A firework fizzles and cracks overhead. I squeal with child-like delight, and we cower as the sparkles drizzle upon us. He takes my hand and we run to safety. Our eyes shimmer in the coloured glow. We laugh. He turns my head towards him and kisses me. I weave my arms inside his coat, and he wraps me up; my frozen cheek rests on his chest, and he strokes my hair. Everything is perfect in that instant.

We drink hot chocolate from the dining hall vending machine and sit out on the steps, engulfed by others sharing our evening.

"It's getting late," I say, as he stretches out on my floor and gazes up at me.

I paint my toenails pure blue, like the deepest of oceans; the glittery specks serve as the sun glinting on the serene surface. I almost smell the far-off summer as I apply the polish, although my small heater is turned to maximum and a harsh wind gusts around the courtyard outside. The single tree is battered and weary. Then the rain comes, icy and relentless. I shut the curtains and the sudden intimacy of the room hangs thick and crushing.

"I wish I didn't have to go," he replies.

I sit to begin the second coat. He tries to reach out to me, but he gets in the way and I have to shrug him off—he might smudge the varnish and I'd have to start again. This is a precarious time, because I'm leaning over my leg, with my knee digging into my breast, and yet I am still trying to be accurate.

"Do you love me?" he asks from my bed, exhausted and content.

I fold myself into the curve of his naked body and stare at the discoloured ceiling. I hope he doesn't catch my sigh, my uncertainty, my anguish. Why can't I answer? His arms loosen; his smile fades.

"Goodbye," he says, standing dejectedly at the door. His shirt is untucked; his hair is more unkempt than usual. He leaves a small Christmas-wrapped present on my desk but doesn't look back at me. He shuts the door quietly, and my room is empty and lost. I open the present when I can no longer hear his footsteps echoing on the cold lino of the corridor.

It's a ring, with a ruby set inside the band. A ruby, my birth stone. *For someone special*, says the card. No one's ever called me that.

"Yes, I love you," I say through the frosty January air as he sits inside with a red-lipped blonde from his Media course, who laughs at everything he says and leans close, touching him distractedly like I never did.

Yes, I love you, and I wonder why I found it so impossible to say before.

They share books and write silly things in each other's notepads. His eyes glance at hers with tormenting tenderness and his hand strokes her face, like he so often did to mine.

"Yes," I whisper again, my breath dancing on the air in front of me. "I love you and I'm a fool." The wind whips around me, but I don't feel it. I'm paralysed where I stand, unable to withdraw, peering through the window, until my tears cloud my view.

Out of my greyness comes baby pink. Women are coy, pouring over absurdly large Valentine's cards. A few of the senders are unknown; the hunt begins. I see *him* in the corridor, receiving a kiss from his blonde; she's holding a large pink card and smiling brightly.

"Hey Pixie," he calls.

We're not strangers, so I turn instinctively, expectantly; and he laughs with his friends. They pat him on the back as though he's done something remarkable. I do not laugh. I feel my eyes burning; and I can see he's noticed.

I stare only at him, and I say, "Yes, I love you."

He doesn't laugh anymore, either. We stand and scrutinise each other, unable to pull away. I feel my ruby ring through my glove; and I wish he knew I wear it, and that when I look at it I think of him until my stomach knots and my heart beats painfully. His friends fade away and we are left alone. I think of all the dreams I've had which have started in this way. I think of all the things I'd like to do and say.

But we both walk away without another word.

I kick through the hail, crunchy underfoot, my toes be-coming numb because I've been out here so long, walking in circles outside his halls, which are nowhere near mine. *Hey Pixie.* I ignore the voice because it's a whispered delusion. It's been calling me day and night, but I refuse to listen anymore.

Then I feel his hand on my waist, a gentle touch like no one else's, and he's behind me. He holds out an Easter Egg. "I bought you this." He bends hesitantly and kisses the back of my neck. He wraps his arms around me, enclosing me in a tight muscular circle. "Can we start again?" he asks as dawn breaks free from black clouds and casts watery shadows across the campus green.

Beth

First, there was a girl. Beth: an ordinary girl. An ordinary girl, extraordinary. A girl who believed she could fly. And she could. Or she could have; with golden hair floating on the breeze behind her, and pale arms and legs swimming against the rippling clouds. *Could have*, if she'd tried, if she'd surged ahead and broken free and forged the place in the world she truly deserved.

But she didn't try, not hard enough. She sauntered, dawdled, eclipsed by the insignificance of others. She slowed down, chose to conform, anchored herself; certain her destiny would be fulfilled in spite of herself.

Then there was a boy. An ordinary boy: just ordinary. He couldn't fly, so he didn't try. He didn't soar or plummet, didn't electrify or astonish. Didn't do much at all. But he worked hard, worked well, plodded resolutely on without looking either left or right. That's how people spoke of him: not as fun or energetic or inventive or sexy or tantalising. *Billy? Ah yes, he's a solid boy, a hard worker.* Someone you'd take home to your mother, and she'd love him from the start. He knew his limits and he was happy. He didn't realise how much of the world was waiting for him, how much there was to see, if he chose to. He was happy.

Then there was a party, where they met. The party Beth didn't want to attend, the party she was dragged to, *just for an hour, then we'll leave, I promise.*

In a dark corner she collided into him and spilled his drink; and bought him another, to be polite. And he tumbled, into a vat of lust and awe and ferocious longing. She smiled and danced, teasing his every emotion, playing; enjoying his adulation. He watched and never wavered, staring only at Beth, shining and beautiful under the lights. His first temptation.

She danced because she knew he was watching, her arms high above her head, her body swirling. She danced because she hoped he'd walk towards her and scoop her up and steal her away. She wanted him to make her every wish come true. And they'd dance forever, just the two of them, extraordinary.

But instead he watched, and when she was finished dancing, and the room was emptying and the lights returned to full brightness, he allowed her to leave.

And she walked slowly, so painfully slowly away from him, trying not to look back. And when she'd very nearly disappeared out of the door and out of his life, he called after her. He rushed towards her when she stopped and turned, hardly noticing the triumphant smile on her lips. And he kissed her.

Then there was a courtship. A tentative push, a gentle prod. A slow, inexperienced fumbling in the dark corner of a pub or nightclub; in the back row of the cinema, watching films no one else wanted to; on a bench in a deserted park where they scratched out their initials inside the shape of a heart. Declarations of rampant lust, but never of love. Too soon for love, too guarded and straight.

Beth waited, and wished. But Billy never said it, would never be cornered long enough. She wouldn't say it first, couldn't be so bold, so blatant. So, she waited and grew resentful, her heart melancholy. And she began to fade; fade back, fade away.

*

Then there was a bouquet. Twenty-five red roses, not yet in bloom. And a card which said everything, all at once; ten lines of plagiarised poetry that expressed everything she needed to hear with little effort from him. Blurted out, spat out. Love, devotion, passion. All of it, all at once. Expressing everything.

He caught her unprepared. She breathed the scent of the flowers, read the card, over and over. She showed no one else. She clasped it to her breast and made her choice alone.

She forgave him, understood him, *wanted* him. Too easily, too appreciatively, as though there'd never be anyone like Billy again. Not knowing that *everyone* was like Billy—that there were so many Billies the world was drowning beneath them all.

Then there was an engagement. A party, a toast, a disco; a family affair. The ring sparkled and was presented, held out for approval and attention. The girl at the end of the hand, basked and revelled. So happy, but with a slight, almost imperceptible, sense of dismay. Chains of adulthood looping around her, slowly tightening. A voice, flitting in and out of the congratulations, inquiring, nudging: *Are you sure, really sure?*

Trapped. Sssh, no… not *that* word. Not *trapped.*

It was a new beginning, a new adventure; a happy time, exciting and essential. Beth and Billy: beginning again, beginning together.

Then there was the wedding. A party, a toast, a disco; a family affair. The dress white and sparkling with a million tiny sequins, the train a mile long, spread out down the aisle. The girl beautiful and loved and admired. For the final time. Because adoration never lasts when you remain anchored, and ordinary.

Happy, yet with a shadow of trepidation across her face. A sinking in her stomach as she held out her manicured hand and smiled at the many friends who'd not had the courage to ask: *Are you sure, really sure?*

And the chains grew tighter.

The day ended. The night enlivened with dancing and song, with drunkenness and laughter. Beth's dancing and Billy's drunkenness. He didn't watch her dancing; didn't need to. He had the girl, ensnared. Now he needed a wife and homemaker, not a dancer; not a girl who would fly. Nothing extraordinary.

Then there was a marriage. An extraordinary girl made ordinary; devastatingly, achingly. Cleaning and tidying, cooking and baking, washing and pegging out, while other women glanced over garden fences and graded her clothes for sense and suitability. And so, accordingly, her clothes became more sensible and suitable.

Working hard to pay their bills, to pay debts from their wedding. Resting hard, lounging on the sofa, dozing at the weekends. Playing forgotten; no longer a reason to play, no longer the need. TV always switched on in the corner of the room, and Beth and Billy always watching, eyes glazed.

Pubs and clubs forgotten. Occasionally Beth suggested a walk to their bench in the park, or to a film they *didn't* want to see. She winked when she asked, curling up to him; but he never saw the wink, never heard the mischief in her voice. And finally, she stopped asking.

Marriage settled them. Too much. Too settled. Ordinary.

Then there were some children. A boy, then a girl, and then another boy. Tiny little Beth and Billies to love and spoil. Tiny little replicas of mum and dad to find their feet, to learn how to fly. But Beth tried to anchor them, to tie them down. She couldn't let them fly, fly away from her. The anguish was too great to let them go; the love she felt for them, too encompassing. And she couldn't admit what she'd lost, what she'd *never* had.

They longed to fly, these babies, before they could walk or talk; they knew there was something more, something better. And Beth clung for as long as possible; a growing sense of fear and dismay. But she wasn't strong enough.

Then there was a man. Peering out from the shadows, seeing the extraordinary. Feeling Beth's power and being overwhelmed—by lust, by awe. Such beauty, such perfection; such ties and distractions.

He smiled one day, as they waited in the same queue, wanting the same sandwich as it happened. "You were here first, you have it," she said with a laugh.

"I'll get something else. You have it."

And they bantered, neither wanting to take the sandwich, which ended up forgotten and bought by someone else. They met the next day, and the next. Not by design; or not by her design, at least. She was overcome by the coincidence, and this man merely smiled, his duplicity buried deep.

Within weeks they were meeting by arrangement. Coffee, platonic and enjoyable; lunch, something different within the mundane working day. He was charming and clever, and encouraged her to be extraordinary. He leaned in close with hushed confidences and secret codes. Beth's hand touched his as she spoke, as she smiled, one day. The spark was entirely unexpected.

Then there was an affair. Extraordinary. Beth flew, finally; her wings opening and feeling the heat of the sun for the very first time. It felt familiar, as though she remembered her true self, her true purpose. Addicted, she wanted to fly more, fly further. She wanted to never walk again. And this man was happy to indulge her, happy to watch her and catch her when she tumbled from the sky, landing in his arms and being scooped up.

She was lured, drawn, seduced away. Her world forgotten, her family dismissed from her thoughts in those brief moments of passion that exploded, extraordinary.

Then there was a question.

"If I left my husband, would you take care of me?"

And there was a silence; extended and excruciating, but entirely expected. And after a moment, there was a slow intake of breath, a long exhalation, a deep frown. "No, that's not for me. That's not why I'm here."

And Beth swallowed, and remained calm, and said, "That's fair enough. That's your choice. That's what I assumed." And she walked away with dignity intact. Outside, when she collapsed into the wall and cried, she realised the pain she'd expected him to relieve her from. And knew that it wasn't his place to do that.

Then there was nothing. No note, no clothes, no Beth. No dinner cooking. Billy wandered around the house, dazed and uncertain, confused and hurt. He didn't know of the affair. He wasn't supposed to. He sat, night after night, waiting for her return. But she didn't come. And he grew tired and weary of the wait. And he found an ordinary girl; just ordinary. No dazzle, no shine. The way it should have always been.

Then there was an angel. An ordinary angel, extraordinary. She took to her wings with glee and abandonment; with her golden hair floating on the breeze behind her, and her pale arms and legs swimming amongst the rippling clouds. She stretched out these wings to their full potential, felt the sun warming them, making them live. And felt the extraordinary.

She swooped and dived. Swooped low over the house once hers. She saw the children, no longer children but verging on adulthood and flying away. She saw Billy hand-in-hand with her successor; she felt his love for her diminishing. And knew it was right and proper.

With regret, she remembered the life wasted, the messy end, the body not found in the river not searched. Because no one knew where to look; no one knew she was that desperate to escape.

And the angel circles high above, chasing the sun so that it never sets, so that she can shine, extraordinary.

The Walking Dead

Last night I dreamt about a jigsaw puzzle. It was silver and gold; and when completed it created a picture of angels. But I didn't complete it. However many pieces I gently wedged into place, there were still the same number of spaces. I woke up feeling cold and hollow.

The room is damp and grey, because outside it's damp and grey. With two panes of glass broken, and no curtains, there is nothing to protect the house.

As I rouse myself, a girl is moving around the room, stuffing her thin sleeping bag into a large Marks and Spencer bag. She stares at me, smiles clumsily, then scurries out. I don't know her; I probably won't see her again. No one stays here long. I've been here for six weeks; too long, but I've got nowhere else to go. This place is, at least, familiar; and no one bothers with me.

It's Monday. I like Mondays, the beginning of a new week; they have the same feeling as slipping between crisp, clean sheets after a bubble bath; or writing on a new pad of paper and watching the ink dribble into the grains of the page. I've always liked new beginnings, new things.

An argument in another room is my cue to grab my own sleeping bag and leave for the day. I roll it tightly and slide it into my rucksack. I grab my battered guitar and take a look round for anything I've missed. I climb through the boarded-up gap that was once the front door, and glance pointlessly around. It's not like I'm making plans.

If I walk slowly enough, the indoor market will be open by the time I get there. If I'm lucky Mr Morris will need help carrying boxes of second-hand books and buy me breakfast from the café.

"You remind me of my granddaughter," he said the first time I stopped at his stall and browsed through the books. The stall is in the middle, the warmest part of the market. The other options were a craft stall with far too many rolls of neon wool or the earnest woman selling homemade soap.

"I've got some chocolate here," he said, when I'd perused two full boxes of Jeffrey Archers and Stephen Kings. "Would you like some?"

"No. Thanks."

He held it out to me, but in the end he unwrapped it and broke up all the squares. He took one and left the rest balanced on some of the books. When he turned away to serve a woman, I stole a couple of pieces and walked away. The next day I returned to say sorry. He chuckled softly. "They were all for you, dear."

Today he's waiting for me, chocolate already opened, one square missing. "Morning, dear."

"Hi Mr Morris."

"You don't look well."

"I didn't sleep."

He looks at me for a moment, longing to say everything he's said before; but he doesn't. Instead, he shakes his head, as though I've done something to disappoint him.

"Could you unpack this box for me? My back's playing up. I'm not sure I can bend down today."

"Sure." I stack the books at the front of the stall, subconsciously putting them in alphabetical order. "Why don't you see a doctor?"

"Because they'll tell me I'm old, and then my family will tell me I'm old, and then they'll make me give up this stall."

"Wouldn't you like to spend more time with your grandson?"

"Wouldn't you like to spend more time with *your* family?"

I stop. "I don't know how to go home."

"You ask me to take you."

The books divert my attention. So many of them to be moved and sorted, I pretend I haven't heard him. When I've finished, Mr Morris hands me a bacon and egg sandwich. He simply nods when I thank him, brushing me away gruffly.

You ask me to take you. Would it be that easy? Maybe. Maybe not. But I'm not ready, so it really doesn't matter.

I move to the music stall. Jack is probably about twenty-five, yet he acts and dresses like he's my age. I hang around for a bit. Sometimes he puts me in charge of the stall if he needs to go to the loo. If I sell a CD, he lets me keep the money. Today he's complaining that his girlfriend has left him for someone else. I feel sorry for him, but I can't be sympathetic. I don't know what to say; I think he's better off without her. I met her once; she looked at me in disgust and asked Jack why he bothered with me. I saw her looking at Jack the same way.

When he finally stops talking and sits staring into space, I make my excuses and leave. Where now? It's half-twelve. I wander along the road for a while, watching people as they bustle into cafés and coffee shops for lunch. Everyone has purpose but me. I stop, sit on the wall outside Costa and settle myself to play my guitar. Just along from me is a guy with a handwritten sign asking for money; he's unshaven and his eyes are vacant as though he's not alive—not dead but not alive. I wonder how long he's been living like this—will I end up like him?

It's old and beat up now, my guitar; a present for my fifteenth birthday. When I left, I grabbed it at the last minute; I couldn't bear to leave it. Playing it is my favourite way to spend the afternoon; I forget where I am, I forget everything except the music; pretending I'm anywhere but here, doing anything but this. The music takes over, sending vibrations through my fingertips.

A few people turn to listen, a few people stop and throw a few coins. Some look at me with revulsion; others with pity. I know I must look terrible; my hair is uncombed, and my creased clothes are as clean as I make them with just water. I try to pretend I'm not doing this for the money, and that it doesn't matter if I only get a couple of fifty pence pieces, or the odd pound coin. My favourite fantasy is I'm eccentrically rich.

The truth is, if I don't get money I don't eat, I don't get a drink, I go to bed hungry and stay awake all night hugging my rumbling stomach. When I'm awake overnight, I hear the scariest noises of strangers coming and going. I cover my ears with my sleeping bag, but it makes no difference.

I'm being watched; not listened to, but actually watched with hard eyes and a scowl. Opposite me, sat on a bench, a cigarette in one hand, is a girl. She looks sick, beyond the paleness of normal illness. There's something tragic about her, as though she's forgotten how to smile or laugh. I want to go and talk to her, show her that *somebody* cares. I sit for a moment, then begin another song: Let It Be by The Beatles, this time, a song to make me cry.

The girl is singing along; her lips are moving and her head is bobbing with the rhythm. I smile, but she stares blankly, as though she hasn't seen me.

When it's dark, I go back to the squat. The house smells; there's rubbish on the floor. A pint of milk has been left on the table and gone off. Grime and dust cover the floors and walls and what little furniture remains. There are a couple of old chairs along a wall; the covers have worn thin and the springs sag. This is home. It's not as warm and inviting as my real home, the home I ran away from. My safe bedroom, fresh food in the fridge, my parents waiting for me.

Mr Morris says he'd take me home…

I ran away because I knew best, because I wasn't allowed out, because I hated school. I ran away because I was old enough to be treated like an adult, because no one understood. Because I hated everyone.

And now I wish I was home again. I wish I could tell my mum and dad I love them, and I'm sorry. I wish I had homework, and a bedtime, and pocket money. Mr Morris says he'll take me home, but what would I say to them. I've been gone for six weeks.

33

I go straight to the wall outside Costa in the morning. I'm curious about the girl and wonder if she'll be there again. She doesn't look like the kind of person who'd have other places to be. Stony-faced people in suits come and go, pushing and rushing past me with their take-away coffees in hand. I don't even think about playing; none of these would think to stop and give me money.

Later, when I start to play, two old ladies smile kindly. They fish around in their purses and throw money into the baseball cap I set out in front of me. "Do you know White Cliffs of Dover?" I shake my head and they walk on.

The girl from yesterday is back. She's wearing a long, shapeless jumper that reaches her knees and a pair of jeans that have more holes than fabric. She has no expression on her face, just glancing around with dark brooding eyes, watching everything. She's sitting next to the beggar. She's talking, and he's answering, but they don't look at each other. Their faces etched with grim reality; they barely notice each other.

I play another song; one or two people stop, one or two reach into their pockets and drop coins into my hat. Most of them just walk past and don't even glance at me.

When the town's clock strikes noon I count my coins—£4.68— and wander the street looking in shop windows. I stop outside the electrical shop. There are three TVs in the window, all showing Bargain Hunt. I used to watch it with Mum when I was home ill from school, when I was still young enough for Mum to have to take the day off work to sit with me. She'd wrap me in a blanket and let me choose DVDs to watch all day, except for when Bargain Hunt and the news were on. We'd try to guess how much the items would sell for. I was surprisingly successful.

I choose a different place to play my guitar. The girl and the beggar are *here* now. They sit close. The girl is eyeing me; the beggar is scanning around. At half-past two they steal my money. They run past and swoop down for my baseball hat without breaking stride— a skilful move. I shout and run after them. No one helps me. I lose them in the crowds. I stand with my hands out, asking for help; but faces turn away now, people move away.

My pockets jingle with the coins I collected this morning. Not many. Not enough to eat tonight. My eyes prick with tears. I can't cry, *won't* cry; I won't let them make me cry. I sit and stare at the faceless people in black, the people who didn't help a starving girl recover her money. I want to stand and yell at them and make them look at me. Instead, I start to strum my guitar and sing another song.

A woman and child are passing by. The child stops and looks at me. She points and asks her mother, "Why is that dirty girl sitting on the ground?"

The mother looks embarrassed and takes the child away by the hand. The girl looks back over her shoulder, eyeing me suspiciously; her mother adamantly doesn't look back.

Stupidly, I allow my own mother to filter in. Stupidly, I think of her and Dad pacing the house, waiting for my return. I imagine them falling asleep on my bed, breathing in the smell of my make-up and favourite body spray.

It's been six weeks since I left. It seems longer. The first few days were hard, before I met Jack and he pointed me to the squat. I've grown up a lot. I've learnt how to stay alive; a skill I'd never needed before. It was harder than I'd thought; in fact, I'm not sure what I expected. But I couldn't go back. Not then.

It's getting dark. I'll go back to the squat soon. I try to stay out as long as possible, but once it's dark, it's not safe around here. People creep around in shadows, hiding in corners and alleys. All the other houses around the squat are derelict too, full of people who wouldn't care if I screamed; who wouldn't step outside to find out what the noise was. I am alone.

There's a pay phone across the road. I feel an overwhelming urge to hear mum's voice. My mobile's long gone—lost or stolen, I can't remember. I search for a coin in my pocket and hold it in my hand, playing with the ridged edge, feeling the impression of the Queen's head on the flat surface.

I hold the receiver to my ear and listen to the purr of the dialling tone. This is a bad idea. I want to hang up. I keep the receiver to my ear, and punch in the numbers. The ring pulses through me.

"Hello?" Mum.

I can't speak. My throat closes over, catching my voice. I force myself to do something, to *say* something. But I can't. My stomach is heavy; I want to be sick. I'm dizzy and have to lean against the wall to keep myself from falling over.

"Hello? Is anyone there? Hello? Are you okay?" Pause. "Who is this? Answer me." She's beginning to worry. And then a whisper, "Jenny?"

I hang up immediately. A shock to hear my name spoken out loud. I stumble over to a bench and sit with my head in my hands. I feel cold and isolated. Even in the rush hour, with people pushing past me on their way to their bus or the railway station, I am alone.

Today, I don't go back to the squat. Today, I walk back towards the market, back towards Mr Morris's stall. Today, I'll ask him to take me home.

Open Windows

Jackie? Hey! Wait for me!" he shouted above the hectic hum of the city rush-hour, on the other side of a four-lane road.

"Michael? How did you find me?"

A lorry drove past and he was lost for a second. He was gone and maybe I'd imagined him.

"It doesn't matter. We have to talk. Stay there."

He watched for an opening in the stream of traffic, dancing on and off the kerb. I was almost numb as I waited for him to grab me and twirl me around like he used to. Suddenly he was running across to me.

He didn't see the car. It happened too fast. A yell. A screech.

Then silence.

Everything stopped.

People ran towards him. I stared, falling to my knees.

I jolt myself back to reality. It's still so vivid; still so painful. At night, in the darkness all alone, I see him lying in the road. I can't get to him; I'm losing him. Reaching out for him. People pushing past me. Everything so silent.

I sat on the kerb, bewildered and lost, everything happened in slow motion around me. Someone was screaming; I think it was me.

After that, I don't remember much. The stark white hospital and endless corridors. The hours and days; the police, my friends. The frosty, tormenting funeral. Just bits. Disjointed.

He died two years ago. And yet he's still here with me, sitting next to me, watching me. Sometimes I talk to him; he talks to me. Why did it have to be him? Of all the people in the world… of all the people I *didn't* love. We would have got back together; that's what he was there for, I know that. It was a stupid row, an argument about nothing, everything dragged up; we said things neither of us meant. But I walked out. Six months later, he found me. Then he died.

We met at an office party, under the mistletoe. It was love at first sight; I didn't believe in it until it happened to me. He was dressed as Robin Hood. I'd started the evening as Rapunzel but with a slight alteration I was Maid Marian. He bowed with a flourish and said I was the answer to his dreams.

Without pause, he flashed a roguish smile and whisked me off to the dance floor. We were inseparable all night. We were inseparable for the next year and a half.

"Hey, Jackie. Are you going to the Christmas party?" Suzie is opposite me. The bright, sunny girl who'd replaced Michael… *who'd taken his job*. Sometimes, if I look up quickly, she *is* Michael.

I realise I've been sitting still, staring blankly as memories seeped into my mind. I blush. "No," I say quietly. "Are you?"

She nods. "I've got a great Rapunzel outfit."

I feel pain shoot through me. It sticks in my stomach, then spreads out again, slowly. I blink and turn away.

At lunch time, I sit alone. I prefer it this way. The others seem too flimsy, too giggly and gossipy; too shallow, too trivial. Don't they realise one day they'll have to grow up, be forced to grow up?

It's my birthday, says Michael.

That pain stabs me again. "I know."

I'm twenty-seven, he says.

"I know," I whisper. "I haven't forgotten."

I was thinking about last year, I was thinking…

"Shut up! Just… shut up and leave me alone." Then I stop. "No, don't go."

I can feel his eyes on me. I wish I could reach out and touch him, smell him and hear his voice. I wish he could hold me tight and tell me everything's going to be all right; I wish he was here. I wish he'd never gone away. I wish a thousand new things every day.

Do you have a pencil? Michael asks from his desk.

I throw the pencil; it clatters onto the floor. I stare at it for a moment, then go and pick it up. I forget he isn't real anymore. Not real… Like an invisible friend. Like I'm a child who needs to make things up. I stand in the middle of the office and look around as though seeing it for the first time. Nothing is as familiar as it should be. I imagine Michael's arms around me. I imagine him smiling.

The journey home is tedious. Too many people jammed into the bus when I want space; nobody around when I need the company. In the summer it's too hot, the winter too cold, yet someone always opens the window as soon as they get on. Never an in-between; never a just right. I never noticed these imperfections when Michael was here. Now I see too many.

I know what's happening. I see myself in the mirror looking old, worn, beaten. I see myself not caring. But it's my choice. This is how I *want* to be.

My mother hates seeing me like this. She doesn't visit anymore. Sometimes she phones, and sometimes she sends clothes: bright colours – yellow, orange, red. She says I shouldn't wear black all the time, she says it puts people off, frightens them, scares them away. I give these new clothes to people who need them.

She sends food too; parcels wrapped in brown paper containing cheese and chocolate. She thinks I'm too thin, not eating, starving myself. I can't remember the last time I was hungry.

I was given counselling when he died. My mother said it would be a good idea; she didn't think I was coping. I told the therapist what he wanted to hear and was let off early for good behaviour. I wasn't mad; I didn't need anyone telling me what to think or do.

So now everyone thinks I should be fine. But it's only been two years.

"You weren't even together," said Janie, as though that mattered.

"It's been six months," Emily said, emphatically.

And then, later: "It's been a year."

Finally, the last time I saw her, "It's been eighteen months, Jackie. Let's book that trip to America."

They think I should forget him; find someone else to love.

"Not *forget*," said my mother, when she was still coming to see me, "just move on."

I don't want to move on. I want to stay here.

Back home, after battling commuters who today were numerous and intrusive, I open a bottle of wine. To Michael. Happy birthday.

I sit on the floor, lean against the living room wall. I don't think about anything. I clear my mind of everything and let myself drift. It's so much easier not to think. I watch the car headlights shining on the ceiling as they speed past. I watch the lights until my eyes hurt.

I stand at the window and open it. An icy blast attacks me. I peer out; the ground is a long way down. I hold onto the window ledge tightly, scared that if I let go I'll fall, or jump. But I don't close it. I stand there playing some sort of dare game with myself, letting go with first one hand, then the other, then both together and leaning forward just a little bit further.

His birthday. Twenty-seven. We'd made so many plans; we thought we had forever; we hardly had any time at all. I pour another glass of wine and gaze at the photos of Michael all over the walls, carefully framed, carefully placed. He isn't smiling in any of them. Somehow I never managed to take a photo where he was smiling.

I reach for my laptop, looking for a picture from his last birthday before he died. He was smiling in that one. I was sitting on his lap, my arms wrapped around his neck. I remember he was smiling in that one, but I can't find it.

You don't need to see the photo; I'm smiling right now.

"Yes. I do."

I continue to search through the folders. They all have labels like Christmas 2010, Dad's 65th, My Leaving Do 2008. And yet I can't find this one photo. It's not even in Michael. Two weeks later, we argued, and I left. If I'd known… I flick through the photos, pour more wine. I wake up on the sofa at midnight.

It's freezing; I left the window open. Michael has gone. I'm alone, and scared. Again. I hate the dark. It reminds me how much I need him. I stand at the window, my hands stretched out to close it, but I pause. I wonder what it would be like to jump, to feel the wind rushing through me, to feel the abruptness of the ground hitting me body. I wonder what it would be like to be with Michael again.

Today the world is going to end.

That's what they said on the news. A group of people have hiked up a mountain in Italy, to be closer to God for the Judgement. If Michael was here, he'd laugh at them and we'd go out to the cinema. Now, though, I hope it's true. Then everyone will be equal.

Today I will spend my time waiting for the world to end.

Omelette

The café is quiet today. Just a little further along the road a sign says *Road works starting today and lasting two weeks*, so Josie thinks that must be why. Around the corner, across the busy main road, the hospital rises high over the other buildings. Josie, as she pushes open the café door, glances over her shoulder at the grey imposition and shudders.

"Hello," says the waitress. "The usual?"

Josie wavers; she's never had a usual before. She's never had a local pub where the staff pour her drink as soon as she walks through the door; never even committed to a regular newspaper, or a favourite Starbucks coffee. She feels bolstered, but at the same time it means she's been eating here too long as she bides her time between hospital visits.

"Yes. Please."

"Just plain?"

Josie looks up at the menu hanging above the counter. "Yes. Just plain. Thank you." She walks to the table in the corner, opposite the large window. *Her* table. She slips her bag from her shoulder and glances at the paintings on the wall, noting the tiny price tags attached to each one; noticing them for the first time, which means she mustn't be so distracted today.

"These are good. Whose are they?" she asks when the waitress brings the omelette, plain, salad garnish on the side, no chips.

"Mine," the waitress mumbles, blushing slightly.

"Do you sell many?"

She shakes her head. "No. But I don't mind. I'd miss them if they weren't here."

***

"Hello," says the waitress. "The usual?"

"Yes, please." She hesitates, wondering whether she should make conversation. She did yesterday, so is it expected today? Once there's a connection, are you compelled to continue it? To be truthful, Josie doesn't feel like talking; she wants to sink down into her own concerns. There's an awkward moment, both equally unsure what to do next, then they both drift in their separate directions: Josie to her table, the waitress to the kitchen.

Josie sits on her hands, feeling the warmth of her thighs bring a tingle to her frozen skin; she's forgotten her gloves again, perhaps she should have them sewn inside her coat after all. That was Meg's suggestion, when she gave them to her for Christmas; Meg knows her too well. Josie sets her mobile on the table, so she can answer immediately if it rings. She sits on her hands and waits. The mobile doesn't ring or beep. Which is good. She doesn't want it to ring, or beep, that would only bring bad news.

"Here you are." The plate is presented—omelette, plain, salad garnish, no chips—an exact copy of yesterday's lunch, and the one before that, and the several before that.

"Thank you." She stares at the plate.

"Are you all right? Is the omelette okay?"

"I don't think I'm very hungry."

"Perhaps you've just had enough plain omelette?"

Josie looks surprised at the idea of another kind of omelette on her plate. She shakes her head. "I've been to visit a friend in the hospital. She's getting worse not better. She was supposed to be coming home today, but she's not well enough. I was supposed to be…" She stares down at the mobile, frowns, reaches out for it, but changes her mind. "I don't want to go home without her."

"How long have you known your friend?"

"Forty-two years, roughly. We were at primary school together. We were supposed to grow old together."

"You still might?"

Josie wipes a tear from her eye and smiles. "We still *will*," she says defiantly. She picks up the fork and half-heartedly breaks off the first mouthful of omelette.

***

There's a space on the wall. Yesterday there was a seascape on the wall opposite; a beautiful red sunset, a yacht pushing off into the distance. A perfect calmness on a vast sea. Yesterday, Josie stared into the painting and imagined floating away on that ocean. Floating peacefully away.

"Oh, that lovely painting's gone, the one with the sunset." Josie indicates the space, the wall faintly scarred with grime, marking out where the frame had been.

The waitress blushes. "I sold it."

"Congratulations. I liked that one. I'll miss it."

"Thank you. It's the first one I've sold."

"Then you should do something special with the money."

"I'll probably just pay the rent."

Josie looks across the room at the wall. The empty space feels ominous.

"How's your friend?"

Josie shakes her head. "Not good."

"Are you hungry today? Would you like your omelette?"

Josie pauses. She thinks of her plain omelette; she thinks of Meg not getting better. "Actually… um… could I have a mushroom one today, please?"

"Of course. I'll bring it over when it's ready."

***

"Cheese omelette, please."

"Good choice. That's my favourite. I'll throw in some chives, then it'll be perfect. You seem happier today... Your friend?"

"Meg's doing well. Rallying, the doctor said."

"That's good news. She's lucky to have you visiting so much. It must be helping her, knowing you're there for her."

Josie shrugs. "She'd do the same for me."

It takes a few moments—sitting and settling, with the smell of omelette already wafting from the small kitchen—to realise there's a new painting on the wall. Two bubbling white-haired ladies sitting on a bench, laughing like schoolgirls, while wind whips their headscarves and tips their shopping bags.

"I hung it there for you, for your friend."

"You painted it for me?"

The waitress looks sheepish. "Well, no. I had it at home—it was something I painted ages ago. But when you told me about your friend, I remembered it. I thought it would cheer you up."

"Thank you." Josie smiles—a thin, wistful smile. "That's such a lovely thing to do." Her eyes are drawn back to the picture, lost in this world that might never happen. "It's breast cancer, you see, what Meg has. She was in remission. But she's..." Her voice shakes a little.

The waitress is unsure how to react. Hesitantly she reaches out and touches Josie's arm. She moves away, clearing a table close by; not wanting to leave this poor woman completely alone, glancing back at her every so often.

The café isn't busy, not since the road works started—a few people are dotted here and there, either talking in couples or reading books and newspapers alone. Only Josie looks around, aware of her environment, opening herself up. She looks out of the window, noting the start of another downpour, the sky darkening, the roads glistening. She glances at the headline on the newspaper left behind by someone. A politician up to no good; a celebrity illness. None of these things properly register.

Her gaze returns to the picture on the wall, again and again. There are tears bubbling, but she's smiling as well; a soft smile, a slow sad smile. She leaves the omelette half-eaten. She leaves the café and walks out into the rain.

***

The waitress watches the clock. At one o'clock she tells herself Josie is running late. At two o'clock she fears Josie's friend has taken a turn for the worse. And at three o'clock, she convinces herself that she upset Josie too much by hanging the painting of the two old ladies. The waitress finds herself standing in front of it, imagining being sat on that bench with an old friend, oblivious to the world passing behind them.

When she painted it, she had no one in mind. The two friends were just inventions; they appeared as if by magic, fully-formed on the canvas. Now it seems intrinsically linked to Josie and her friend. And yet she wishes she'd never brought it in. She stares at the painting, trying to view it subjectively; astonished that something she'd created could affect another person so much.

At five o'clock, the waitress turns the OPEN sign to CLOSED. Heavy rain is falling again, car headlamps sparkle off the road, and people scurry past under hoods and umbrellas.

***

Today is Saturday. Saturdays are different; routine is suspended, the vibe is different. Fathers in weekend disguise with their boisterous kids; friends meeting for a day's shopping; lovers recovering from their romantic Friday night dinners. Everyone is light and relaxed, happy to linger over an extra coffee and share a slice of Death by Chocolate.

Josie doesn't come in on Saturdays, so the waitress knows not to glance expectantly out of the window. A busy day; a non-stop day. The waitress coasts above it, unaware of the variety of people queuing behind each other, unaware of their stories, unconcerned.

Nothing matters today; she's drained of curiosity.

The painting—untitled, but in her head now called *Josie and Meg's Day Out*—still hangs on the wall. She thought about taking it down, but it's there for now. Why does she care so much? Why has this woman, Josie, affected her, when so many other people who come in daily don't even register? She places two cups of coffee in front of two women with several shopping bags wedged on the chairs next to them and can't even remember the last time she went shopping with a friend. She can't remember the last time she saw a friend, other than at work, or passing in the street and dashing onwards with hurried promises to call. She never does call. She never has the time. Time doesn't last forever though, does it? Josie doesn't have time.

She imagines herself lying in a hospital bed, linked up to wires and monitors potentially keeping her alive, and wonders who would visit her.

***

Monday again. Another week. Another grey and miserable morning.

Josie stands in front of the painting, striding across to it rather than standing at the counter and ordering. She senses the waitress cross the café to join her. She feels the warmth, the companionship.

"Can I buy it?"

"Um. Yes. Of course."

"Isn't it for sale? I thought you said they were all for sale."

"It is… they are. I just… I thought…"

Josie turns, curious, concerned.

The waitress blushes. "I thought I'd upset you by putting the picture up."

Josie softens. "No. I love it. Meg's dying. They've only given her a couple of weeks. I wanted to buy the painting for her. I wanted to show her how it will be, in my head."

"I'm so sorry." The waitress looks away. "It's a present. Take it."

"Oh, I couldn't. Don't you have rent to pay?" She chuckles uneasily, then notices the waitress's earnest gaze. "Thank you."

***

Josie reads the menu, but none of the options match how she feels today. She wants colour; she wants to feel uplifted and revived. Peppers and spinach and tomato: colours of a rainbow filling her plate. She makes her request timidly, unsure whether she's required to adhere to the menu.

The waitress smiles. "I'll see what I can do."

"Meg loved the painting, by the way." Josie raises her voice slightly, so the waitress can hear her from the kitchen. She glances over her shoulder to make sure the other diners aren't disturbed by the noise. "We cried a lot."

A head appears around the opening. "Oh, I'm sorry."

"No, it was *good*. We said everything we needed to say, we said goodbye I suppose. I think she's ready now… prepared, you know." Josie's voice drifts away, her gaze softens. "She never had kids, she got divorced a few years ago and never met anyone else. She just kind of existed alongside everyone else. Makes you wonder why she was here at all, doesn't it?" Her face drops, horrified that such a thought could have entered her head.

"No," says the waitress quickly. "She was here for you, and for all her other friends. And even for her ex-husband. As soon as you meet someone, you've affected them. You and me —we've made a difference to each other, even if we don't realise it yet."

Josie takes a long breath. On the verge of tears for Meg and for saying goodbye, she can't contemplate the philosophical view right now. "Well, I guess I eat different types of omelette now."

The waitress pauses, with a flicker of a frown, then smiles. "It'll be ready in a moment. Take a seat."

Josie plays with her mobile, pressing buttons to watch the screen light up. She waits for the call, hoping it won't come. She checks to make sure the ringtone is audible. She stares at her reflection in the dark screen.

"Do you really believe what you said before, that we all make a difference?" she asks when the omelette arrives. She didn't mean to ask such a thing, but she couldn't help herself.

"Yes."

"How have you made a difference?"

"That's not for me to say."

"But you think you have?"

"I know I have. I *must* have." The waitress hesitates for a second, then sits down opposite Josie and rests her hands flat on the table. "When I was little—six or seven, I suppose—I used to scare myself by looking at the stars. You can see hundreds, thousands of them. The more I looked, the more I could see. Have you ever done it?"

Josie shakes her head.

"On really clear nights you can see the Milky Way… and the world—when I was six—suddenly seemed so small. And I thought, if the world is that tiny, then I'm a speck, even smaller than a speck, totally insignificant in this great, massive universe I couldn't even begin to imagine. So, I chose to believe that I *do* matter, that everyone matters." The waitress leans back in the chair and laughs at herself. "And, yes, I realise it makes no sense at all, before you say anything." She stands and smooths her apron. "Enjoy your meal."

The waitress steps backwards, pausing as though she's going to say something else. But she's drawn away by a new customer. Josie watches her smiling and laughing easily with this new person in a way she's never done with Josie.

Perhaps, Josie thinks, she fosters melancholy in others. She's not always so glum. She laughs with Meg: or rather, Meg forces her to laugh. Even now, in agony in her hospital bed, Meg jokes with the nurses, reminiscing with visitors; cheering up others when they're overcome by the reality of it all.

That's the difference Meg has made to Josie. And it's a good difference. Without her humour and buoyancy, Josie thinks she would have sunk into a deep depression. Her encompassing gift for worry and distress would have driven her too low to ever rise up and be happy again. She fears this will happen anyway, when Meg is no longer there to support her.

***

"Which one today?" asks the waitress, tempering her mood to match Josie's.

"Just plain?" No, not plain. Meg asks her to describe her meals now that she can't eat—how could she make a plain omelette sound exciting? "No. Tuna. Please."

"How's Meg?"

Josie looks grim. She smiles weakly but shakes her head. She can't talk. She turns away and sits at her table, glancing out of the window briefly. She puts her head in her hands. The air is heavy around her, pushing her down. She feels sick now; the smell of food cooking is churning her stomach. When the plate is set in front of her, she looks at it and doesn't know how to begin.

Then, faintly at first, her mobile rings. She stares at the waitress. The waitress stares back.

Shadows of Autumn

It's autumn. Autumn again. I stare out of the window and feel sorrow for the departing summer. The trees look so mournful; with their branches running like spilt ink into thickening grey skies, reaching out, craving that last scrap of sunshine, that last embrace of warmth. Discarded leaves litter the ground. All colour is absent, forgotten.

Everywhere is dark, heavy. I'm pushed down, choked up, stifled.

I turn away, weary. I puff out my cheeks and let the air flow through pursed lips. I don't feel like reading; there's nothing on TV. It's dark now. I close the curtains, turn on the lights. Puff out my cheeks. I survey the empty room as though some-thing might have changed when my back was turned. But it hasn't; everything is just the same.

Alan will be home soon, walking through the front door with deliberate, even steps. I sit and wait for him, patiently; like a devoted dog who waits beside comfy old slippers and the evening paper. I sit and do nothing but wait, blank and hollow; nothing else to do.

The pictures on the wall bear down on me. The faces watch me; judge me. Hanging on the wall for people to view when they visit;

hanging there so I don't have to remember each individual moment. Happy, smiling faces. Such fun times: too many to remember.

Too hard to remember.

But then, of course, these visitors—these people storming my house—feel uncomfortable as they realise who they're looking at, and smile with tentative sympathy. Today, even these photographs are harsh and critical. I listen to the strident silence.

The knock at the door makes me jump. I peer through the curtains and see a police car. When I open the door, two officers stare back at me: one man, one woman.

"Mrs Howard?" says the male officer. "Is your husband at home?"

"Er, no, he's at work. Can I help?"

"We'd like to speak to the both of you, if that's possible."

"Is he in trouble?" The thought is ridiculous before I even say it. Alan is too staid, too correct; I can't imagine him ever doing anything wrong.

"No. It's nothing like that, Mrs Howard," the woman intervenes with a compassionate, apologetic smile. She leans forward slightly, showing she's in charge. "Will your husband be long? Could we come in and wait?"

Suddenly, I realise. "Oh my God, oh my God..." How stupid of me. My heart thumps inside my chest; I feel faint and lean against the door. I should have known; I should have guessed. It should have been my first thought. "It's Nikki. You've found her? You know where she is?" The sound of her name is alien. I haven't heard it spoken aloud for several months.

"It really would be best if Mr Howard was here as well?"

"She's dead... She's dead, isn't she?" I'm whispering now. I hold my hand against the door frame to steady myself.

They don't answer; they look at the floor, stare at their feet. We look at each other, all of us, just looking.

"You'd better..." My legs buckle beneath me, and two pairs of arms hold me upright. We stagger towards the living room and I sink into the nearest chair. I lean back, exhausted.

"Will Mr Howard be much longer?"

I glance at my watch. Half-past six already. Sometimes he's home by now; but other times… There's no way of knowing. "I'll phone him." I reach for my mobile, dial, and wait for his dull voice to answer. I ask him to come home; I tell him to come quickly. He doesn't ask why, so I don't tell him.

They sit, the police officers, side-by-side, perched on the settee opposite me. They don't talk; I'm not sure what I'm supposed to say. They look unsettled, staring their hands resting on their knees and with brief glances at the photos on the wall.

My mind is numb, like a shield has been placed across my eyes and I can't see, can't react to the things happening around me. I always thought Nikki would still be alive; hoped that she'd have found a place to be happy again. Grown up and happy.

I always dreamed that she'd come home.

The photos are all of her. I'm in one or two, Alan's in a few; but mostly it's just her. It makes me feel as though she's still here—just popped to the shops with friends, just left for college, just gone out on a date. I look at them now, my eyes fleeting from one to the next, then the next. A pretty girl. She takes after her father: blonde hair, blue eyes, tall and slender. People never believe I'm her mother, because we look so unalike. I expect she's changed by now, though. Grown her hair, or cut it. Got taller. Her face become more angular, more adult; although she's just a child. Still my child.

If it's autumn, it means it's been four years since Nikki disappeared. Four years since my Nikki…

I said *disappeared* again, didn't I? It's a lie, of course. It's what I tell everyone who asks; it's what I tell myself because I can't bear the truth. I can't admit it was my fault, that I was to blame. I can't bear what that would do to me.

She left, you see. Nikki left. My Nikki. Of her own accord. One day here; the next day gone. I never thought of myself as a bad mother. But I must have been, because she left.

There was a note on the kitchen table when I woke up that morning. Just one line, and her name printed neatly after it. I can't even remember what it said, the note which had lain on the table all night. Alan held it in his hands until the pencil was smudged and he couldn't read it anymore. He still has it, somewhere, tucked away. They were so close. It broke his heart.

Her friends knew nothing, so they said. They didn't know why she'd gone; didn't know where she might be. Didn't know who she might be with. Because, of course, she must be with someone, mustn't she? Someone who'd convinced her he loved her and whisked her away. She'd be back as soon as the glow of first love had diminished. Wouldn't she?

One friend came round a few times, sitting with me while we waited for news, letting me know if Nikki's social media accounts updated. But they never gave any clues; and after a time, there were no more. Then the accounts vanished. The friend stopped coming by. Everyone began to move on. New friends to make, the new year at school, exams, college. Nikki *who?*

Alan blames me. I know he does. He's never said so; but I can feel it. He moved into the spare room soon after she went, making some feeble excuse about not sleeping, not wanting to disturb me. Did he think I was sleeping? I still hear him shuffling around in there; I still lie awake listening to every single sound. Endless nights lying in bed, tracing the shadows on the ceiling, waiting in the darkness. I miss him just as much as I miss Nikki.

That's why he works late. That's why I had to phone him tonight, to drag him home. He works as much as he can; it keeps him away from me.

It's my fault; and I can't remember what I did. Said no when she wanted to sleep at her boyfriend's house, aged fifteen; asked her to load the dishwasher; suggested jeans instead of short flimsy skirts and towering heels. I may have asked her to be home by eleven on Saturday night.

All the things I was supposed to do. All the things other mothers do.

We sit in silence, the police officers and me. Not even a ticking clock to distract us. I offer tea or coffee. They refuse, politely. All the police I've known have been polite. I've known a lot.

Time stands still. I rock backwards and forwards. It comforts me; it's like being back in the arms of my own mother. It's what I'll do when Nikki comes back to me. Rock her slowly, gently. Backwards, forwards.

The front door opens. Alan calls, "Hello?"

He walks into the living room and sees three pairs of eyes staring up at him. We all stand simultaneously. A glance at me. He places his hand on my shoulder, warm and heavy. I shiver because he hasn't touched me for so long. He doesn't say anything, but he knows. He realises much faster than I did; and now he's scared. He looks at the policeman and waits.

"We've found… a body." The policewoman steps forward a little. "I'm very sorry." It's always the women, isn't it? On the telly, it's always the women who give bad news.

I close my eyes. They feel scratched and swollen as I try not to cry, trying to be brave in front of Alan. Boiling tears slide down my cheek. One at a time. I'd hoped—so hard—that she wouldn't say those words. My head starts to spin. Alan's hand squeezes tighter.

"The girl matches the description we have of Nikki. We need you, Mr Howard, to… to identify the body."

I breathe deeply. "What happened?" I find myself asking, watch myself asking. "To the girl… what happened to her?" My stomach is heavy.

"We need to establish if the girl is Nikki before we can share any details."

I let out a whimper. It must be bad. They're trying to shield me. I let them. My legs fold beneath me again. Once more, I'm escorted to the chair.

Alan puts his briefcase on the floor and moves towards the door. "I'm ready now."

"I want to go too."

He comes back, crouches beside me as though I'm a child, holds my hand in his; they're shaking. He leans into my line of sight, his eyes soft, a little blurry with tears. His face is ashen. "It's okay. I won't be long." He glances at the policewoman. "You'll stay with her, won't you?" She nods. Alan kisses my forehead before I realise what he's done.

Then it's just me and the policewoman, Karen. I try to speak, but the words catch in my throat. I sit, rocking. Backwards, forwards. I'm so cold shivers run around my body.

I have this picture in my mind of Nikki, when she was about three. She's looking at me and laughing, a tiny dimple in each chubby cheek, her eyes are lit up, she's so excited. It's Christmas. We've given her a doll's house; it's almost as big as she is. She points out each tiny doll and every meticulously-detailed table and bed. She shows us the windows and doors that really open, gasping with each new discovery.

We've told her to be careful with it, so her chubby fingers are hovering but not touching. Her face is full of amazement, as though it was the most magical gift in the world. Alan lifts up the baby's cot and shows her the baby inside. *Just like me*, she whispers in awe.

Did she think I was a bad mother then? Did she hate me, even then?

Karen catches my eye, says something reassuring. She must see this so often. Yet she can never really understand what I'm thinking right now, what any mother is thinking; each one suffering her own unique pain. I take a deep breath. It quivers. That's me. *I'm* quivering.

What happened that day? And the next? What happened the week after she wrote that note and left the house for the last time? Did she find somewhere safe? Did she have something to eat? Did she take enough money? Was she scared?

It can't be Nikki. I'd feel something inside, wouldn't I? I'd know. Nikki's part of me. She came from my body. I'd *know* if a part of me was dead.

"Would you like a cup of tea?" asks Karen.

"Yes, I'll…" I try to stand. I stumble, fall back.

"It's okay. I'll get it." She touches my shoulder briefly as she passes.

In the kitchen, Karen clatters crockery, opens cupboards, tries to find her way around. It jars into the silence. I walk to the other side of the room, take a photo from the wall: I hold it and stroke Nikki's face through the glass. I think of Alan. I remember his warm hand on my shoulder. I remember his kiss, so tender. So familiar, yet so illicit.

I still love him. I don't know if I should. People, some people, don't expect me to. I find that strange—he's my husband; and he lost a child too. I don't know if he loves me anymore. I've often felt that as soon as we find out about Nikki, one way or the other, he'll leave; just pack his bags and say goodbye. Right now, in this limbo, we need each other. But soon...

"She's pretty," says Karen, appearing behind me, two mugs of steaming tea in her hands. She startles me.

I'm still holding the photo. I pass it from hand to hand, put it down, pick it up. "She *was*," I correct her. I put the frame back on the wall, adjusting it so that it hangs upright.

"It might not be Nikki."

"You must think it is, to put us through this."

She looks at the floor. "Sometimes we're wrong," she mumbles, nervously. No, I think, you never think you're wrong.

"You can't always be wrong. It's still somebody, isn't it? It's still somebody's daughter." I gaze at the photo. "Why do they have to grow up?"

Karen shakes her head. "I bet our parents wondered that as well."

"You have to let them go though, don't you? You can't keep them as kids... I wanted to. She was so beautiful. But you have to let go, let them make their own mistakes. I wish I could have..." I stop, sigh, draw back from the wall. "I suppose not."

She says nothing. I can feel her eyes focused on me. What is she thinking? Does she feel sympathy? Does she blame me as well? Answer me! Do you think I'm a bad mother too?

"Does it often take this long?" I ask. I've always hated waiting, despite all the practise I've had. But it's been so long already, does this extra hour make any difference? I'll know by the end of the evening. I'll know soon enough.

"It depends. Your husband might have wanted to take time before... you know"—a deep breath, an exhalation—"before going in."

Or he'd want to take his time before coming home, before having to tell his wife.

I sink back into my seat, sipping the hot tea. She's put sugar in it.

I don't take sugar; it tastes like syrup. Maybe she thinks I'm in shock. You do that for shock, don't you? Or that might be something else. I sip at it, trying to ignore the taste.

Four years. Autumn again.

It doesn't feel that long; it feels as though I've slipped from then to now without taking anything in, without the months passing, or seeming to pass. Stuck in limbo, hiding from the world.

"When Nikki was younger," I say aloud, needing to hear some noise, "she hated being away from me. She'd scream the place down when I took her to playschool. I had to sneak away once she started playing." I take another sip of tea. "It sometimes feels as though she's dead already. Everything's empty."

I wipe a tear from my face. "I was looking forward to having grandchildren."

Nikki's only eighteen—why am I thinking about grandchildren? I stare at a spot on the carpet over by the coffee table; I picture her playing with toys, cross-legged, absorbed.

Karen shifts in her seat; I notice her again. "Do you have children?"

"A baby. A boy."

"I wanted a boy, a little brother for Nikki. It never happened." I frown. "We wanted another child… but you can't argue with nature."

My mind goes blank. It decides it doesn't want to think anymore. I look at the photo of Nikki directly in front of me—another one, a different one; from Christmas, aged ten, Santa hat and cheeky grin—and refuse to cry. No, I *want* to cry. I want to show Karen and Alan, and anyone else who has an opinion, that I do—that I *did*—care. Do they realise how much of me vanished that day? Does Alan realise that I'm feeling exactly the same as him? Does he know how much I love Nikki?

I hear the front door open. I look up, apprehensively. Alan and the policeman talk in low voices in the hall. The living room door opens. Alan stands there with his eyes red and blurred, his face white and drawn. I don't know how to react; I don't know what he's going to say. I inwardly practise different emotions. Outwardly, I stare, fear spreading icily from my stomach.

He says nothing, does nothing, just stands.

Karen and I wait. No one moves, no one speaks.

Alan's voice cracks. "It wasn't her."

He walks back out of the room and into the kitchen. He turns on the tap, fills the kettle. I follow. When I reach the kitchen, he's standing with the full kettle in his hands. I watch him. He seems uncertain what to do. I take the kettle away from him.

"It wasn't her." He's crying. I've never seen him cry. Not even when Nikki first went missing. He held it all back, or he'd leave the house; or he'd shout. Shouting and shutting me out, that's been his survival. Hiding himself away. He steps across and hugs me tightly, holds me; his arms so strong around me, so safe and soothing. "It wasn't Nikki," he repeats.

He wipes a tear from my face, kisses my forehead, holds me close. My head rests on his chest.

Portrait of the Painter

Jo is eating bread and butter. Or rather, she's spread the butter on so thick she's eating a butter sandwich. Just the middles, not the crusts; she leaves the crusts at the side of her plate, like discarded chicken bones.

She licks the butter from her fingers, each one slowly in turn, already distracted by her next thought, then wipes her fingers across her painting shirt. She leans back, studying the canvass closely, adding a line or mark, an extra touch of colour here or there. She's sitting cross-legged on her years-old IKEA rug, with her paints and brushes spread out around her.

These seemingly careless strokes are the distinction between an unexceptional painting and a work of genius. Jo wants to create genius; her art is her entire life. *I wish I could paint like that*, people whisper to each other in galleries where the work is shown. Jo pretends she doesn't hear.

"How much longer?" asks Simon, getting restless.

Jo smiles and glances over the top of her canvass. He's balanced on his hands and knees, one arm held in the air. Jo wanted him to look like a tiger, roaring resoundingly, ready to pounce on his prey, powerful and strong—a study of the animal inside the man. Well, that was the idea. Instead, he looks like a soft tabby cat who wants to snuggle into someone's warm, comfortable lap. She'll add black and orange stripes to the human flesh and improvise the roaring part.

"Hush. Hold still. Not long now."

He's been like this for the past three hours, on and off, while Jo perfected his eyes, his mouth, his jawline. Next she moved to his body, his forearms and thighs. Simon watches disheartened as she continuously crosses out a part of him and starts again. His arms beginning to sag and his shoulders start to hurt; he can no longer feel his legs at all.

Simon didn't realise it would be such hard work; though he couldn't really have expected anything less than crawling around semi-naked on Jo's hard living room floor pretending to be a tiger. He only agreed to do it because he's in love with her, and if he hadn't said yes she'd have found someone else, who was also in love with her, instead. Not on purpose. Jo doesn't think anyone is in love with her, or ever could be.

Jo had black hair when Simon first met her. It's red now, deep carnation red. In the right light—late at night when he's walking her home across the common, and the moon is hidden behind rain clouds—it looks almost purple. Every so often her natural washed-out brown colour shows through when she can't decide whether to dye it again. Those times, she buries her hair into a hat, or pulls it tightly into plaits. She always *does* dye it again, in the end. She always dyes it red.

It's long, Jo's hair, flowing down her back like a waterfall. She tucks it behind her ears when she's considering her next colour or brushstroke, or she winds it around itself and stabs it with a pencil to keep it bound together. The ends are usually speckled by paint at the end of the day

Simon remembers the exact time and place they met: Jo doesn't. She says it was too long ago to even think about it. She looks away in disgust when he mentions it, glancing back and smiling tenderly at him when he isn't looking.

"We were at college," Simon says to the mirror when he's alone, pretending people care that he's friends with this great artist. "I was on a business studies course. Jo was doing English literature. I'd seen her around, of course; it was impossible not to notice her. All the guys were madly in love with her, but she never noticed any of us… any of them. She glided around the corridors totally unaware. At lunch times she'd sit alone under one of the trees, gazing off into the distance."

Here, too, he'll gaze away, as if trying to recall, a contemplative smile on his lips that will betray him. Those images are etched firmly in his mind. "I first spoke to her on my nineteenth birthday. She dropped a book on the path. I followed her and gave it back." Of course, they—these fantasy interviewers—will ask if he ever slept with her, but he'll just smile again and refuse to answer.

That long. They've known each other that long… Simon can't believe it. He can't believe he's almost thirty, doing the same job, living in the same town—the same flat even. He wants to be more like Jo; to get up one morning and decide not to work that day, to catch a train to the coast instead and spend the afternoon sitting in wind-battered cafes on the cliffs.

Once, she phoned him, after not seeing him for a few weeks and said she was in France. She was bored one day, so caught the ferry across. She was staying at a camp site near Toulouse. "I'll be home for Easter," she shouted as the signal bounced in and out. "Make sure you buy lamb. I love lamb at Easter. I'll be there by eleven."

What would it feel like to spend the whole day in bed, or go shopping, or to the cinema on a Thursday afternoon when everyone else was at work? To go on holiday whenever you want, suddenly, without telling anyone, because you can. To not be trapped by a job you hate. To not worry about tomorrow.

He can't do that though. He does worry; he worries for the both of them. About his job, money, the future; about not worrying. And he worries about Jo. And Jo just laughs at him, telling him to calm down and relax. He wonders why they're friends, why she likes him, why she's stayed around for so long. And then he worries that one day she won't be there, she'll get up and leave and not come back.

*

Jo looks up, gazing around before focusing on Simon, as if she's forgotten he was there or why he was there. "Would you like some music?"

"I need a break." He stretches his arms above his head, growling when she asks him to keep still.

"Just a second longer." Her hand slips easily across the page. She pauses, peering at the canvass through half-closed eyes, pushing her fringe out of the way. She opens her eyes again and smiles. "There. Okay, you can get up for a minute."

"Can I look yet?" Simon's stands and stretches, unfurling limbs that have been immobile. He groans as the blood starts to flow again. "I know: *it's not finished yet*," Simon mimics before she has a chance to answer.

She sticks out her tongue and threatens him with a brush covered in yellow paint, waving it inches from his body. She catches him on his leg; he grabs her hand and lifts her to her feet. He twists the brush around in her hand, almost touching the tip of her nose with the bristles. She lets out a small squeak and stares up at him. So close, Simon can feel her breath on his cheek; he steps back quickly.

"So," says Jo, looking away casually and swirling the brushes in water, her face glowing red, "how's work? Still wearing a suit?" The first time she saw him wearing a suit was on his first day in his first job. She bumped into him in the high street during his lunch break. She'd burst out laughing, more as a defence than anything else. He'd looked so different; powerful and sexy; he took her by surprise.

"Work's fine. You still looking for a job?"

"I don't need a job. Not at the moment anyway," she adds softly, bursting with her secret. "I sold another painting, that's my fifth now. And the buyer wants another one." She grins, anticipating Simon's reaction.

"That's fantastic. Well done. This one?"

Jo shakes her head slowly. "No, not this one. Mr Curtis," she says with a childish pout, "would like a landscape. He would like me to paint him some hills." Her smile falters, and her eyes narrow into an expression of hostility. "I mean, the guy buys Matthew and commissions a landscape! Why not just go and take a photo!" She stabs her foot at the sofa, and winces.

Matthew is a naked man, wrapped in cling-film. He's holding the Earth in both hands, his mouth wide open as though about to bite into it. There's a red tinge to the world; Jo wanted it to resemble the poisoned apple offered to Snow White.

Jo scowls, wishing she could afford to paint what she wants to paint. People who aren't shocked by her work anger her.

"But, that's two sales, Jo. I know you don't think you need money, but you do. You can't live like a student forever."

"I don't live like a student." But she glances uneasily at the scant furniture scavenged from charity shops, and the threadbare rugs hiding even more threadbare carpets. She doesn't own a TV and her computer is Simon's old one. In the fridge right now, she has a quarter of a pint of milk and an egg.

"Come on," Jo says abruptly, "back to work." She folds herself back down onto the floor and waits for Simon to find his position again, instructing him to move his head a bit to the right, up a bit, move that arm, stop, back a bit. Stop. Hold it. That's great.

Jo enjoyed college at the time; though now she wonders why it was so important. She was just starting to paint then, after discovering a Wednesday evening art group. Suddenly it was the only thing that made her happy. She was Josephine until then, of course; or sometimes, Josie. She likes being Jo; she likes the simplicity of the word. She can be anyone she wants to be because Jo doesn't give any clues.

She told Simon, early on, that she was a painter rather than an artist because the thought of him imagining pots of emulsion being splashed onto the sides of houses was amusing.

When she first showed him her work, he was stunned. He stared, caught up with the colours, the fantasy; he understood the meaning in each one. And she knew, at that moment, she would always paint. She needed to experience that reaction again.

At times, Jo feels like giving up. She decides it's pointless, that she's kidding herself. She feels as though she's pretending to be an artist, an adult, and soon she'll be discovered as an imposter. She'll be forced to wear her hair in pigtails and play with the little boy down the road; forced to eat her crusts because they'll make her big and strong. She'll be forced into the life she ought to be living.

She contemplates everything she's accomplished and sees nothing of merit. She sees a mass of painted over canvasses thrown into the corner in anger; she sees half-completed notebooks full of half-conceived idea. She wonders what it's like to be normal, to not live in a vacuum, to go to an office on Monday morning and leave her work on a desk on Friday evening, to see friends at the weekend and eat proper meals rather than cobbled-together snacks when she remembers. She wonders whether she's wasting her time. At times Jo buries her head and hides.

Simon likes watching Jo work. He watches as she scoops her hair from her face, twisting it around itself at the back of her neck. He watches as she leans back and contemplates, then reaches forward, straining forward to the far corners of the canvass. He likes the way she's so wrapped up in her work it seems that paining is the only thing she really cares about. She's different to the women he's dated who are simply interested in making an impression on people. Jo makes an impression without realising.

He watches her as she watches him, scrutinising his face, his body, his arms and legs. He feels her gaze resting lightly upon him, the warmth in her eyes. He wants to feel special, but he knows she's not really seeing *him*; she's only seeing the image she wants to create.

By now, he hoped he'd have moved past this stupid desire for her, this unrequited love. He knows he's wasting his time. Jo is whole. When he looks at other people he sees them as one half of a pair, incomplete, waiting for that perfect fit. To put Jo into a pair would be to dilute her.

Once, just once, Jo told Simon she loved him. He felt like the only man alive; although she never said it again, and she probably only said it because she was drunk anyway. But for that one moment, as Simon held her hand, he was happy.

*

Jo sings along to the radio, swaying back and forth in time with the music. The trickiest part is over now. Simon has been captured and soon he'll be able to get dressed and make dinner for the both of them, clattering comfortingly in the kitchen as Jo perfects the sky or the grass.

When she told Simon she loved him that time, what she really meant was that she needs him, because he's the only person she can turn to when she feels scared and alone. She feels scared and alone a lot. What she really meant was that he makes her laugh and cry and feel good about herself, good about her painting. She meant that… that if he ever left her, she wouldn't know how to cope. She wishes she could explain this to him, but she doesn't know how. So, she's painting this picture of him, and hopes he'll guess.

Every so often she stops singing, crease her forehead, chews on the end of the paintbrush, makes an alteration on the canvas and smiles again.

The Girl who is Good

The girl who is good sits between her parents in an elegant restaurant, doing and saying very little, and being very good.

She's nineteen here but could easily be mistaken for fifteen or sixteen. Her head is bowed throughout the meal as her parents talk to each other in muted voices, peering around her as though she isn't there. She eats nothing. She considers her plate, pushing food back and forth. Once or twice, she takes a sliver of lamb or a slice of carrot and moves it to her father's plate. She stares at him as she does this, daring him to stop talking for a microscopic moment and finally notice that she's there. But he doesn't. They don't.

The girl who is good visits the Ladies three times during dinner. The first time, she does nothing but stare into the mirror at the stupid pink bow her mother made her wear, at the childish pink gingham loops that she wishes she could rip from her head and tear into pieces. Instead, she washes her hands and pouts; her eyes darkening with fury, instantly replaced with icy serenity.

The second time, she looks forlornly into her miserable reflected eyes, and shoves two fingers down her throat and brings up her starter. And then she feels very good. Her eyes shine a little brighter; her mouth almost, ever so slightly, smiles. She revels in the lightness of her body, the clawing emptiness.

When the girl who is good visits the Ladies and looks so bleakly into the mirror, it's me she sees. Me, with a glint in my eye. Me, waiting to break free. The girl who is good sniggers doubtfully: I've been making these absurd promises of wickedness for so long the words no longer have meaning.

"Right," says Father, slamming his hands down onto the table with what is meant to be jollity but seems officious and controlling. "Onwards." He raises his hand for the bill.

Onwards. Yes. The part of today I've been truly dreading. Father has unearthed a husband for me, and we're meeting him this evening. My father expects me to be grateful and comply with his superior acumen. He doesn't use the word *husband*, because that would be reminiscent of an arranged marriage; and *of course, darling, there's absolutely no pressure whatsoever, we just want you to be happy. We just want to introduce you to new people.* He uses *suitor* instead, and I feel positively Georgian.

I haven't asked where this *suitor* was unearthed; I imagine a business acquaintance of some kind. I imagine meetings at the golf club over a few drinks, a few effortless hints of the spinster child at home. I imagine self-congratulation between the fathers and plans for business already drawn up.

I excuse myself from the table one last time. I lean on the sink and gaze into the mirror—the inevitability is a burden—and yet I still purge my body of the very last morsel of food.

***

The housekeeper escorts us to the library, and Mother is impressed; I can tell by the slight rise of her nose, the re-adjustment of her shoulders, the pat of her hair with both hands. Mother is a snob, and Father knows exactly how to get his own way. Neither is truly thinking of me right now. Mother is already arranging the wedding and imagining the grandeur of the guest list.

"Mr Faulkner has been held up at a meeting. He'll be home soon. Can I get you anything to drink while you wait?"

We sit in silence sipping sherry, which I hate, which Father always requests—ordering for me without asking. The alcohol is going straight to my head due to the lack of food and the room is slightly swaying.

Mother browses the books that line the walls. I'm at the window and looking both outside at the silhouetted tress and back into the room via the reflection. I'm oppressed by the sombre mahogany dresser, the forest green leather chairs; I'm appalled that the room seems to have been decorated to suit the idea of a library. It's cold and soulless. Hopefully, it's a much-used room; books shouldn't be left to perish.

Father is looking increasingly nervous. He stands, sits, rubs his hands together, paces the room, and taps his foot on the wooden floor. I watch him as though from a great distance. He doesn't look like my father, with this inverse window view. He's almost a stranger; and I begin to realise he's also a stranger when I look at him the right way around. We used to be close, until I was about seven or eight. I'm not sure whether it was me or him who changed.

By accident I catch a glimpse of myself. And even I look like a stranger, hollow and sad in the warped glass.

The sound of a motorbike skidding on the gravel attracts my attention outside. A beautiful shiny Harley Davidson Fat Boy snarls up the drive. A leather-clad figure slides off. Maybe it's him. Maybe Father hasn't told her we're meeting a biker; a Hell's Angel? Oh, *please* let him be a Hell's Angel.

The figure walks into the library a moment later, helmet tucked under his arm. Oh, never mind, it's his father. This guy's about forty-five, with greying hair that's curled into the shape of his helmet. His face is tanned, rugged rather than wrinkled; he smiles easily, and I need to catch my breath. He pauses briefly, nodding at each of us, then drops the helmet onto the table and strides across to Father.

"James," he says warmly, shaking Father's hand, "I'm so sorry I'm late, conference call with the Aussies." He turns to Mother.

"And Mrs Grayson. How lovely to see you again." He steps towards her and kisses both cheeks lightly.

"Have we met?" Mother looks from him to Father, and back again. Her smile ripples but remains in place. She hates being at a disadvantage.

I watch, still via the window. No one's noticed me; I'm just an observer now.

"Christmas. A few years ago," says Father, dismissively. "Henry. It's a pleasure."

The girl who is good steps from my body, leaving me at the window to fade into the walls and curtains. She's smart and clever; courteous and polite and all the things I'm growing to despise, all the things *I'm* not. And adults love her.

"When will your son arrive?" the girl who is good asks during the clumsy pause after the pleasantries have been shared.

"My son?" Now Henry looks uncertain.

"Ah," says Father, "perhaps I should explain…"

And immediately everyone understands perfectly. Except for, perhaps, Mother, who glances around waiting for illumination.

"You mean," she says slowly, and I can see a flicker of realisation, "you don't have a son? *You* are the man we've come to introduce our daughter, our little girl…" She coughs away the escalation in her voice. Her eyes widen. She commands a benevolent smile. "Well, obviously my husband has made a mistake." She shifts her weight from one foot to the other, fiddling with the clasp on her handbag, uncertain of the etiquette.

In my corner, hidden away, I laugh, making ineffectual attempts to stifle myself. The girl who is good hears me but pretends not to. She visibly bristles and assumes her superior expression. I want to slap her face, hard enough to raise the shape of my hand. Instead, I just laugh again, contrived and cutting.

Henry stares straight at me. I hold my breath and become very still, pushing myself deep into the wall. I'm not supposed to be here, by the window; I'm supposed to be over *there*, in my body. He frowns a little, glancing between me and her. He smiles, his eyes softening.

"Would you like a ride on my bike?"

Mother is half-way through explaining the impropriety of Father's idea and frowns deeply at being interrupted in such an ignorant manner. She opens her mouth to protest. She turns to Father in a *do something* kind of way. But Father merely sits by the open fire and pretends to warm his hands.

I nod with a wicked grin, and he holds out his hand for mine. Mother and Father and the girl who is good watch with mouths wide open as he turns and says, "I'll send Juliet to freshen your drinks." And he guides me past them all and out into the chill evening air.

I stand beside the Harley stroking the frosty chrome, smoothing down the black leather. Henry eases the spare helmet over my head, and straddles the bike, steadying it while I clamber on with much less grace. Mother watches from the window. I can feel her without even looking.

"Will they be angry?" Henry asks, suddenly concerned.

"Oh yes." But I slip my arms around him and hold tightly so that he knows I don't want to go back. I can't go back. The girl who is good would never let me forget an abortive attempt at rebellion.

Out on the road we accelerate until the hedges on either side become nothing more than a blur, until my body feels liberated and insubstantial. I scream with excitement and fear. I grip securely, my arms wrapped around Henry's slim, firm waist. I lean into his back and close my eyes as we speed faster and faster.

I don't open them until we stop.

We're not back at the house, as I'd assumed. We're on the side of the hill about five miles out of town with a halo of orange light pollution rising above it. Circling the town, villages are scattered as if by accident; their lights are whiter and fewer. In between is empty. I stare hypnotised until Henry touches my arm and indicates for me to remove my helmet.

"We won't stay long, it's too cold. But I thought you could do with a breather before going back to face your parents."

"Do I look like I need courage to face them?"

He doesn't answer because the answer is *yes*, and what kind of stranger would say something like that on a first meeting.

He's right, of course; I do need a breather. I do need to gather my strength. Because they won't be happy.

They'll smile through clenched jaws when we return and make polite small talk through drinks. They'll ask pointed questions about our excursion and seethe all the way home. Because I am the girl who is supposed to be good. And girls who are good do not run away.

"Did Father think he was bringing me to meet your son? Did he misunderstand?"

"No. He thinks you would be the perfect wife for me, because you have the beauty and I have the money, and I think he'd be much happier living two hundred years ago when these things actually mattered."

"They both would." I shrug despondently. They don't hide the fact they think I should give up college and get married. They both think I should have babies, and a large house. I think they'd love for me to live in Henry's large house, with his housekeeper and cook —and his money.

What I actually want to do is move to London with my friend Lizzie and rent a tiny flat and wait tables to scrape together enough money to travel the world and never come home. I want to work in New York and Morocco and Australia.

"Are you looking for a wife?"

He smirks a little. "Not particularly."

"No… I'm not looking for a husband either. But I don't seem to be getting much choice at the moment."

"They just want the very best for you."

I grunt. "Are all adults programmed the same way?"

"You're nineteen, you're an adult yourself."

"But I don't want to be." I wonder what the girl who is good would say if she was here, what kind of comments she'd make to fill the silences. "Do you have children?"

"I do have a son, actually. He's seventeen. He lives with his mother in France."

72

"Oh." I can think of nothing else to say; he's giving no clues. So I rest my head on his shoulder and we stare out across the town.

"We should be getting back," says Henry after a while.

I lift my head and feel a crunch in my neck from being in the same position for so long. I consider all the things I'd rather do. "No, not yet."

"Don't be silly, they'll start to worry."

"Well, then, let them worry." I pull myself further into him. I slip from the bike and stand in front of him, my hands lightly resting on his waist. "Have you ever been bad?" I whisper, leaning forward and kissing him, brushing his lips. In the fading light, I can't see his reaction.

He folds his arms, blocking me out, pushing me away. "The fog's coming in. We'll have to go."

"No. Not yet," I repeat with a soft purr. "I want to stay here all night, with you. Aren't the stars beautiful? Aren't there so many?" I reach forward again, trying to ease myself into his arms. "Wouldn't you like to stay?"

He pauses for a moment. "No. This is silly. We have to go."

"We don't have to do anything we don't want to." I frown. People—well, men, I suppose I mean—never say no to me. They say *no* to the girl who is good, because she doesn't ask the right questions.

"Get on the bike, now."

I stiffen. He sounds like Father. "No."

"I'm going."

"I'm staying!"

"I'm not leaving you here."

"Then you'll have to stay too," I sing-song. I take a step backwards, away from him; and another, and another; until I can barely see him. The blackness and fog blur him. "Come on, come and catch me."

"It's freezing. You'll catch a cold."

"Come and get me." I laugh aloud, anticipating the chase.

"We need to go."

"Go then, I don't care. It's so refreshing out here." I'm still walking because I know he'll follow. He says nothing. He's creeping up behind me, ready to pounce and tickle me, and make me scream. The ground softens beneath me. I have left the path of compacted mud and veered to one side. My hands brush against the tall grasses and bracken.

"Come back." His voice is suddenly so far away. There's a catch in his tone. "I can't see you."

I've twisted and turned in the fog and can't tell which way I came. I answer his fading entreaties. He calls out; his voice, straining with urgency, evaporates before it reaches me.

"Henry! Henry! Where are you? I can't see you!"

So faint now. Just a murmur; just an echo bouncing on the thick air. It seems only a brief moment before I hear the revving engine, wheels spinning on the gravel track. Leaving! He's leaving me behind. I try to run, but I don't know which way to go. I stumble on a rock, fall to the ground. I can see nothing at all in front of me, behind me, above me.

The fog creeps on, enveloping me, curling in on me. I've lost myself. I close my eyes without fear, without panic. I'm safe and calm. Like drowning, I allow myself to be carried along, to twist and turn, to rise and fall with the contours of the hill.

The girl who is good laughs; she glances out of the window and feels my pain. I'd like to think she cared enough for the darkness outside to hold her attention. But, of course, after a while she'll turn back to the group and sit silently while the adults talk around her, being very good. Mother will be charming; Father will be standing with formality at the large fireplace, sipping his sherry.

I imagine the possibilities; the life I can have now I'm no longer chained. And it's a good life.

Tasting the Grass

There is a special smell to grass. Wet grass; wet, early morning grass. Fresh, unspoilt; almost overpowering.

It's this smell that wakes me now, wakes me up from a dream of dragons and knights in shining armour. I wake up feeling different, as though everything has changed overnight, as if nothing will ever be the same again. Then I remember… it *has* changed. Everything has changed. *I* have changed

I glance across at the slumbering shape lying next to me in my bed. A wonderful, glorious shape. A shape I want to spend the rest of my life with, to wake up next to every morning. Is it possible to be so in love with someone you don't even know?

No! Stop. This is all wrong. It shouldn't be like this.

Maybe I'm still sleeping; or maybe I've woken up in someone else's body. That would explain it. Maybe that's why I feel this way. The shape beside me is a stranger; maybe very well known to the person whose body I've stolen, but not to me. I shouldn't be feeling this way.

There's someone else in my life, you see. Someone who is not this shape in my bed. She loves me, and I love her. I tell her I love her; have I been lying to her? I guess I must've been, or why would someone else be in my bed? Why would this man be in my bed?

He stirs. I hold my breath. I watch the seconds ticking slowly on the clock. *Please don't wake up.* I can't face him yet. I want to watch him sleep, curled up like a child cuddling his favourite toy. He's harmless when he sleeps. I don't know what will happen when he wakes up. I don't know what he'll say.

Now I'm scared. He might panic, he might realise he's done a very stupid thing and want to escape as soon as possible; he might not even remember my name. No, he can't leave. I want him here with me. I want him to stay asleep in my bed.

Oh, what have I done?

I've been with Amy for three years now. Practically forever. This would kill her. A man! I'm considering leaving her for a man. Why would I leave? I've only known him… glance at the clock… I've only known him for twelve hours. I can't even make coffee until he wakes up; I don't know how he takes it.

I used to do this all the time before I met Amy; meet someone and plan our future almost immediately. I was scared of being alone; anyone seemed better than no one. I believe in snatching what I want. I grab everything: lovers, jobs, the last chocolate biscuit in the packet. No matter what.

It works sometimes. Other times I get hurt; and my friends shake their heads, and hug me tenderly, and tell me I'll never learn. My friends say that's what makes me *me*, and they never want me to change. All I want is to stop getting hurt.

Mark. That's the name of the shape lying next to me. Mark. I say the name to myself, breathing it softly. Blond hair, damp with sleep, stuck to his forehead; ice blue eyes, cold and cutting, except when he smiles—when he smiled at me last night—and they seem to glow, to light up and change colour.

It's getting lighter. The sun begins to seep through the gaps in my curtains. A soft breeze flows through the open window.

He'll be awake soon. Mark… he'll be awake. And that's when this dream will cease to exist. I'll cook his breakfast, he'll thank me, say goodbye and walk away. And never come back. Why should he?

He'll just see me as a one-night stand; not exactly a mistake, but not something to be repeated.

Or he'll run out of the house, collecting his clothes on the way and not stopping to find out where the nearest bus stop is. He'll be totally repulsed and want to be as far away from me as possible; to get home as quickly as possible and shower my smell off his skin.

Or… not. How can I judge want he'll do? I don't know him. He's just a man I met. And maybe that's how I'll remember him in the future—*just* a man.

I think I mentioned Amy to him at the beginning, when we were sipping cocktails at the bar and making idle conversation. We both forgot about her later, when he asked me to dance and we found a dark corner. She didn't matter; she wasn't important. Oh God, she'll always be important, she will always matter. I don't know what she'll think of me now. If I don't tell her, someone else will. Maybe, just maybe, she'll have done the same thing once, and understand what I'm going through. Or she'll hate me.

Sliding out of bed, I creep silently across the room, glancing back at Mark. I feel a sudden spark of energy shoot through my body, settling deep in my stomach. It shakes me; I give a muffled yelp. Mark doesn't move, doesn't hear. I hold my breath and wait. I feel nervous in my own house, as though I don't belong. I wonder what he's dreaming about, whether he's dreaming about me.

I shiver. I realise I'm naked and throw on my dressing gown, feeling the soft silk dancing on my skin. I sit at the dressing table, studying myself in the mirror. My hair is getting long, I'll have to get it cut soon. Amy likes it long. Her hair never grows past her shoulders, she envies me. She likes brushing it, long sweeping strokes in front of the fire on empty winter nights.

My face is a mess. I forgot to take my make-up off. Black mascara smears across my cheek. I look pale and hideous. I wonder what Mark would think if he saw me now. I pull out a face wipe and start to fix the worst of it.

Amy's photo looks at me, with anguish in those eyes which are usually smiling out from the frame. Those beautiful eyes which watch you carefully and know all your secrets. If she was here now, even without Mark lying in the bed, she'd know. I imagine them filled with tears, my betrayal stabbing into her. I flip the frame face down.

The sun is pale through low clouds and there's a light drizzle. And the smell of grass, of course. I can almost feel it on my lips, tasting it. It reminds me of when I was young—well, younger—growing up on my parent's farm with my sisters.

The farm was Heaven to us. We fed pigs, we nursed lambs, and camped out in the small orchard all summer long. But, one by one, they encouraged us to leave home anyway, to go to university or get a job in a city or find someone to settle down with.

Of course, if any of us had been a boy they'd have kept him, taught him; they'd have given him the farm, in due course, which was something at least two of us longed for ourselves. My parents never hid the fact they wanted a boy. That's why they had five of us; they hoped next time they'd be lucky.

I haven't seen my family for years, not since I met Amy. They didn't approve—of her or of me. I knew they wouldn't. But I hoped they loved me enough to be happy for me. They'd be glad to know about Mark, they'd approve of him. I don't care what they think anymore; so I don't need to tell them.

Mark sits up. I watch him in the mirror. His hair is tousled, his eyes bleary. He glances around as though trying to remember. This is it, the moment I've been dreading; the moment I am rejected.

But instead, he smiles. "Morning," he says with a Geordie accent that's so novel and yet so familiar. Then he holds out his hand for me, watches me as I cross the room and lie down beside him.

Knickers and Wellies

Rain pours. A moment ago there was nothing, now it's a torrent. I open the back door and listen to it cascading off the roof. I hear the whoosh, the shlop, the pitter-patter. The air is thick and tempestuous; the sizzling heat lures me outside. I *shouldn't* be tempted; I've still got too much to do. Half-packed boxes are strewn around the house: clothes and boxes and kitchen gadgets I'm taking, even though they're not strictly mine. There are piles of things to be taken to charity shops or thrown away: my things, *his* things.

There are photos of him to be torn up and cried over; there are things to be *accidentally* broken with a smirk.

Despite that, I pull on my wellies and raincoat, and step outside. I wade through the long, overlooked grass and open the back gate. I'm walking down the service lane and out onto the main road before I even realise.

Almost immediately, I'm sticky with sweat and pull down my hood, feeling a brief reprieve as the rain cools my head.

But my body is hot and prickly inside the nylon, so I open the zip and hold the corners of my jacket out wide. The air wafts around me, a little, but it doesn't last; it's not enough. As I walk past the park, I remove the jacket altogether, and I feel light and refreshed.

I think a tear slides down my cheek. Rain or tears: sometimes it's hard to tell the difference, isn't it? I didn't mean to cry again, not out here in public, but it's my default state at the moment, now that he's gone.

Bastard! I hate that he's made me cry, made me miss him so much, made me love him.

My shirt tightens around me, the arms constrict my movement. I try to shake loose, to run away; but I'm thwarted. My clothes make me feel claustrophobic. I'm nauseated at the sensation of them on my skin. The cotton scratches my arms; the denim suckers up, squeezing my thighs. I unbutton the shirt and pull it off me, letting it dangle for a moment from my fingers, then dropping it on the ground.

I walk on: past the primary school, past the chippie all shut up on this Wednesday afternoon, although the aroma of grease fills the air.

I walk on: past the swings where a mother is trying to extract her child, while the child clings to the chains and screams loudly. *But it's raining*, the poor woman tries to reason. The screaming continues and as I walk on, around the corner, along the street, I can still hear the shrill screech.

I walk on: ignoring the thoughts that are running through my head, ignoring the urge to hunt the bastard down at his new girl-friend's house, ignoring the impulse to walk into her bedroom and pin him against the wall.

By now, my jeans are stiff and unwieldy; the rain is running off them in rivulets and collecting in my wellies. They cling to my legs, pinching them, binding themselves around me like a snake. I unzip the fly and pull them over my hips, down my legs. I take off one boot and inch the jean leg methodically over my ankle. The boot goes back on and the other comes off. The wet denim is hard to manoeuvre. I sit on the low wall of a small car park and concentrate on the task, relishing the release from my fabric prison.

My legs are free. Free to move fluidly and unrestrained; delighting in this new-found world of nakedness. They're warmed by the rain.

I throw the jeans over the wall, and they land a surprisingly long way away, slumped over a rose bush on the edge of the car park, forlorn and discarded. I feel a tinge of regret; they were my favourite jeans before they turned against me, and they were quite expensive. I no longer need them.

A flash of lightening sears through the black clouds, rumble of thunder rolls across the sky, long and low and tumbling. I turn my face upwards and close my eyes. The rain falls against my cheeks.

I am further encumbered. This time, it's my vest clawing at my stomach, clenching itself around my chest, squeezing my breath from my lungs. We fight each other in the middle of the street. I attempt to pull it off me, this bright green vest with its imitation bone buttons and a seam that no longer falls straight; but it clings tighter, holding on the way a baby chimp grabs its mother.

I hear a rip and pause. The seam has torn; the vest whimpers. I haul it over my head in one swift defeating move. I've won. I hold my head high and walk on, the victor. I'm heading towards the town, now, the main shopping street. And slowly I become aware that I'm wearing nothing but a bright red bra, non-matching green knickers and a pair of blue flowery wellington boots. And my skin is mottled purple, reacting to the torrent beating against it.

For a moment, I'm self-conscious and anxious; but then I feel strong and confident, and oh, how I want to see that bastard right now. Oh, how I'd love for him to see my new-found liberty. Oh, how I wish other people knew how to cast off their problems and be as free as this.

Instead, just along from the library, I bump into a group of grey-haired ladies from the WI. I smile with as much composure and triumph as I can manage—I am free and happy, ladies!—but they stare back at me in shock. A couple cover their eyes, another lets out a small gasp and turns her head away.

The rain is dripping across my shoulders and coursing between my breasts, now the vest is no longer there to absorb the moisture. My hair hangs limply, sticking to my face. I brush my fringe from my eyes and say, "Hello."

They stare with stony eyes.

I start to laugh. A giggle at first, as I look at each of them in turn. Then a snort as their shock turns to disapproval. A chortle as their disapproval turns to disdain. A full-on belly laugh when I realise the absurdity of what they're seeing, and I can't stop. I bite my lip; I attempt to explain, but I can't get the words out. Their disdain turns to outrage, and that's my cue to get the hell out of there.

I don't run. It wouldn't be pleasant for me, wobbling down the road at speed, trying to contain two ample breasts in hands not quite big enough.

No, I don't run. I zip along, with a skip every so often, unable to contain my exuberance. Because actually, in spite of those women at the library—or perhaps because of them—I feel valid and vibrant and very alive. All that stuff waiting for me at home, all those boxes and possessions, they mean nothing; not when I'm half-naked in the high street in the pouring rain.

I smile and turn back the way I've just come, breathing in the smell of wet, fresh grass. I've beaten the clothes that were trying to control me; I am free and satisfied. I can feel the tickle of rain drops on my back.

The Guitar at the Centre of the World

The poster promised blue skies and sunshine while a languid audience stretched out on fine lawns and watched an array of musicians and bands. It declared music of an unbeatable standard and a wonderful family day in the grounds of a beautiful manor house. The poster had been displayed around the area for weeks, pasted up on lamp posts and in the post office window.

Today, however, the field is wet, sodden. Groups of people huddle together under red and white golf umbrellas, or they share oversized cagoules. The music began an hour ago: a local band—enthusiastic punk trio entirely inappropriate for half-past two on a lazy Sunday afternoon—who stopped abruptly when rain got into their speaker.

Now we're waiting for a group of young kettle drummers to set up; two of whom have yet to arrive, while a third is having a panic attack in his mum's arms. The others, eleven or twelve of them, are wandering around in matching purple shirts, arms linked to form a large ribbon. Their parents, obliged to spend weekends standing in fields to support this unusual hobby, are bunched together with heads turned towards the beer tent.

Over by a large tree, a family of five shelter beneath leafy branches. The two eldest girls dance to the chart music being piped over the Tannoy; they hold hands and spin around in a circle, faster and faster, laughing uproariously. The baby, no more than nine months old, is being bounced on her father's lap. She giggles and gurgles as Daddy pretends to bite her nose.

"Sit down and eat something," says the mother, overly concerned about the number of sandwiches she made last night. They told her she'd done too many. *You can never have too many sandwiches*, she said; but now she's surrounded by piles of chicken salad, ham and cheese, and egg mayonnaise sandwiches, limp and somewhat grey.

She looks up and hates what she sees. "Don't run. Come and sit down. Mind that lady. Don't roll on the grass, it's wet. Have a drink. Have a sandwich. Mind that lady!" She hasn't enjoyed life since her first child was born; there's too much to do, too much to worry about.

From her bedroom window, the manor house owner's daughter is watching the fun, wishing she could join in. But the manor house owner's daughter is dying—slowly and inoperably—and the family worries excitement may exacerbate her condition. She hates dying; life would be so much more fun without it. It's been happening for a long time, and she's used to these rules that keep her confined. But she wishes that one day she could be down on the grass, getting wet and uncomfortable.

This whole day was designed with her in mind, after all. The stage is placed precisely so she can view it from her window; the bands were booked, mostly, to appeal to her tastes. The kettle drummers, who have finally taken to the stage, remind her of searing hot tropical sunshine and walking barefoot across sand. They remind her of her last foreign holiday, the one just before she was sentenced.

In a moment, her mother will arrive with two large 99s from the van, and they'll settle down to slurp them while they watch. They'll laugh at all the wet people, and joke that they should invite them inside. They'll dance in their chairs, and the mother will glance at her daughter and wish they had more time.

The juggler holds three balls in his hands, then throws them into the air, deftly catching them all in turn, his hands moving so quickly they leave echoes of themselves in the air.

Kids of all ages watch open-mouthed and clap and laugh when he drops them. He kneels down and holds out two soft balls to each of the children. First, he shows them how to throw one ball in the air and catch it with the other hand, watching the concentration of their small faces with amusement. Some of them frown, others chew their lips or stick their tongue out of the side of their mouth; others pout and complain they can't do it before wandering off to find their parents.

When one ball is mastered, the second is introduced. After a few minutes' absorbed perseverance, one of the little girls can juggle for five throws in a row before her hands get knotted up and the balls fall to the floor.

The juggler is a local policeman, a regular visitor to the daughter of the house. He sees past her illness; he sees her vibrancy and humour and compassion. On rare days when she's feeling strong enough, he walks with her around the gardens. She links his arm for support, walking close to him, and sometimes resting her head on his shoulder. He doesn't express his feelings; indeed, he feels as if he's been informally warned by the family not to do so. From her window, the manor house owner's daughter watches the juggler, and smiles.

We see, from the vantage point of the low dry-stone wall to the left of the stage, a mass of people, a medley of colour and movement. Earlier, when the rain first started, they hunkered down, set in, their faces and bodies resigned to the downpour. Couples cuddled up. Or they sat slightly apart, forgetting they weren't alone. Or they sat on tartan rugs with kids lying between them. Or they piled high with friends.

Now they're dancing in the rain, singing along with the Irish band who are having so much fun up on stage it's impossible not to be immersed. Long skirts cling to brown, freshly shaved legs, or are gathered up and knotted on one side; trouser legs are rolled up. Feet are bare. Splatters of mud mark their ankles like intricate tattoos.

From here, everyone looks so small, like toys that have come to life in the nursery. As the field sweeps down and curves away from us, individual people are sucked into a collective, their colours and shapes blended together. And the music grows louder and faster.

The field is an extension to the ornate gardens that are closer to the house; the stage has been landscaped into the centre. To one side, a fishpond has been fenced off. Several children are chasing around this pond, stopping occasionally to force their heads through the railings and stare into the deep water.

The worrying mother, sitting under her tree, watches with rising concern. *Where are their parents? What if a child should get stuck? Who's in charge and where are they?*

A little boy stumbles on a loose paving slab and falls to the floor; his bottom lip quivers before he lets out a loud cry. His mother arrives and sweeps him up into her arms. He's too big, these days, to be regularly carried, but he remembers the connection and re-assurance; his arms and legs curl around his mother like a monkey, determined not to let go.

She smooths his hair and whispers into his ear and makes him laugh through tears. Another whisper and he nods enthusiastically, wriggling to the ground. They join the small queue to the ice cream van, and magically the injury is forgotten.

In a brief reprieve from the rain, when the sun breaks free and a weak rainbow appears, a woman in black discards her raincoat and stands barefooted on the lush, thick grass. She feels the blades tickling between her toes, feels fresh and young again. On the stage, there are four barefooted violinists. They look remarkably similar to the dancing lady—her daughters, maybe, or nieces? Either way, she seems intimately acquainted with the music; she closes her eyes and hums along with a smile on her face. And when the rain returns, she doesn't notice. She simply holds out her arms and turns her face upwards.

A guitar is placed on the stage, and a man wearing a faded Ramones t-shirt uncoils roles of leads and begins to plug in the speakers, the amp, the microphone, and of course the guitar. He moves swiftly, having done the same thing many times before, scurrying across the stage on his knees. Once everything is ready, he sits on the stool, picks up the guitar and begins to tune it. He strums a few bars, makes a few adjustments, strums again. When he's happy, he sets the guitar back in its rack, pats in instinctively and leaves the stage.

People have been watching him because there's nothing else to do as the rain becomes heavier again, landing in fat blobs on makeshift shelters and abandoned picnic boxes. At the back of the field, the juggler has moved on to a fresh bunch of kids, keen to learn and upset when they fail. Their mothers are queuing for henna tattoos; their fathers are at the beer tent casting the occasional eye towards them.

Back on stage, the singer and his guitar are ready. There's no announcement he's about to start; he just sits and starts to play, as if he's alone. All eyes turn and settle upon him. He strums the intro; he closes his eyes and sings. His voice is mellow, soft and liquid. He sings Through the Barricades in almost a whisper so that the audience have to lean forward, and they become trapped within his voice.

The daughter of the house, left alone for a moment while her mother is elsewhere, listens intently with a tear in her eye. Our so-worried mother at the tree abandons her family and walks down to the stage. The juggler glances towards the window and sees his beloved with that beautiful smile on her face. Then he looks down at the faces looking back at him, waiting for the next instruction, and he kneels down beside them.

The singer notes all the eyes turned upon him. He imagines that, as he played his first chord, people outside these gardens stopped to listen, captured by the sound. He imagines that as his voice rises, people further out—in the village and beyond—are turning to the sound. He imagines his guitar has the power to cast a spell upon people several miles away, several hundred miles, so that they all turn to the origin of this perfect sound, the vibration of guitar strings hanging on the air the way a butterfly flitters. And, if hundreds, why not thousands of miles? Why not the whole world stopping, pausing in its relentless surge, as his music ripples around the globe, all eyes turned on him for one magnificent moment?

His song comes to an end. The field is silent for a moment, the air filled with the final lingering chord; the audience entranced by the sound, then they clap and cheer. Another song begins and the singer, once more, is immersed within his music.

My Mother's Mother's Mother

When I get home, I drop the chemist's carrier bag onto the counter, close the curtains and look for the church candle I know I put somewhere safe for emergencies. *Emergencies* being power cuts, hurricanes and the end of the world, as specified by my mother the day I left home. All of these occurrences would necessitate a candle, apparently.

Today, however, there are no emergencies; I'm searching it out for a different reason.

All day I've been thinking about an article I read in Jackie magazine when I was fourteen. On Halloween night, you light a candle in a dark room and place it between you and a mirror. You stare into the mirror and your future is revealed, according to Jackie.

All of my friends had done it and talked about it in whispers at the back of History class. But before I could try it, my mother found the magazine and read it with increasing horror. *Witchcraft, young lady, and nothing less!* Then, to my mortification, she flipped through the pages, and read all the other articles too. Her eyes were wide and appalled as she read the problem page, filled with references to sex and boobs and make-up; her lips pursed, her fingers scrunched the paper.

I hung my head, cringing with embarrassment, and slumped deep into the sofa until my head was at the same level as my knees. At fourteen, my mother still thought of me as ten; worse, she still *treated* me as though I was ten, even in front of my friends. There was no humiliation I had not endured.

I stared at my fingernails and tried to will myself somewhere else. Fury rose within her, rage bubbled. She took the magazine into the garden and set it alight, holding it between her finger and thumb as though it was contaminated. The ashes scattered in the wind, falling to the ground like sinister confetti.

All day I've been thinking about what I might have seen, if I'd looked through the candle when I was fourteen, searching for my future. All day I've been wondering if that one brief incident altered my life so decisively and brought me to this point today. Perhaps if I'd seen my future, I could have taken steps to avoid it.

In the chemist's carrier bag, pushed aside while I continue to search for the elusive candle, are boxes of aspirin and ibuprofen, bought from various different shops due to the absurd rule of limiting the amount you can buy so you don't top yourself.

If you want to top yourself, you buy boxes of sixteen tablets from various different shops.

Don't ask… don't ask why. Some things can't be explained, can they? Sometimes there's no big reason, there's no drama, just many small issues that grind you down until one day you wake up and you cannot move through the weight of every-thing pushing down on you.

Don't ask… please don't ask.

It takes me an hour to find the candle; an idea which turned into a fixation. I couldn't stop thinking about it; I *had* to find it, as though it was the single most important thing I would ever do.

With apprehension, I hold it in both hands; I take a breath and stand still in the middle of the room. I hear the kids next door stamping up the stairs and arguing over a computer game and playing music loud enough for me to hear the thudding beat but not the tune. A dog is barking outside somewhere. I look back down at the candle, and suddenly all of that mayhem evaporates. Nothing exists outside of this house. I hear my heart beating, reverberating around my body.

I sit on the floor in front of the full-length mirror in the hall, with my candle, with a box of matches. Behind me is the unlit dining room, and I perversely recall every horror film I've ever watched; every psychotic murderer, vampire and green-skinned alien is waiting for me unseen in the gloomy corner of the room. *Get a grip*, I tell myself sternly.

And then, in the corner of my eye, I see the chemist's bag again, on the kitchen counter, ominously lurking: my personal bogeyman. I try to forget the contents and take a long, calming breath as I light the candle. It's dark outside; the clocks went back last weekend and now night comes far too soon. The flame flickers into full strength, casting shadows on the walls and on my face. I look through the flame into the mirror.

The room in reverse reminds me of Alice before she stepped into the looking glass. An alternate room; an alternate me. I wonder what she's like, this other me. If she's a direct opposite, she'll be extrovert and idealistic, she'll be lazy and flaky. She'd go out of her way to help a person in trouble; and always try to save people, even those who don't want to be saved. I'd probably find her as exhausting and frustrating as I find myself on *this* side of the mirror.

The flame flickers as I breathe slowly in and out, wondering if I'm supposed to be chanting, or counting down from twenty to zero… or something else entirely. So, I simply look at myself in the mirror, watching my expression alter in the flickering shadows. In this half-light I look quite pretty, though the more I stare, the more distorted I become.

In this yellow glow, I am my mother. I have her nose, slightly up-tipped in disapproval; I have her tight, pursed lips which denote her frequent scepticism or disapproval—her two main reactions. I hadn't been aware of either before, and I don't like it. In this light I also have her sunken eyes and dark shadows. I have the same deep line between my eyes which gives us a persistent scowl. I see the future, my future as a direct copy, right here in this mirror.

My mother missed the sixties by being far too young to enjoy them, and she ignored the seventies because she thought she was too old. Of all the years in the last century to be born hers was probably the worst. In photos she looks incongruous, inserted on top of the action, uneasy and conspicuous, always appearing one moment out of step with the people around her. Maybe that explains why she always seemed so angry with the world; she didn't know where—*if*—she belonged.

Occasionally, walking quietly into the living room or kitchen, I'd stumble upon her staring pensively into space, looking like a surreal portrait of herself. My presence would always startle her; sneaking up, she'd call it. She'd shout her displeasure, embarrassed at being caught so vulnerable; but I like to think in those moments I was seeing the real person. Now, in front of the mirror, I have a spark of sympathy.

My reflection mutates further, and I am my mother's mother. I'm her determination and enthusiasm, her joy and excitement. My grandmother was a spirited woman; people always say that of her—driven to do everything that was unexpected. Marriage curtailed her, too abruptly, conforming her and tying her down.

The way I like to think of her is running, with her hair flowing out behind her, enjoying the thrill of just moving. And then suddenly stopping; suddenly so still and quiet, holding a baby, her new husband stood proudly beside her. A posed, unnatural black and white photo; a posed and un-natural smile.

But there was always a twinkle in her eye, even then, always a sense of mischief that she tried so hard to contain, to curtail. She longed for boundless adventure, encouraging me to shine in her place. I was sixteen and belligerent, confused that I couldn't rebel in front of this woman because that's what she was actively seeking from me.

She rebelled herself, after my grandfather died. She had an affair on holiday in Africa and threatened to move to a tiny village in Zambia. She took up belly-dancing and collected sponsorship for a sky-dive. She protested at the proposed site of a nuclear waste dump even though it was miles from her own home, just so she could be dragged from the assembly and arrested.

"Oh, the sirens!" she says, even now, her face breaking into a huge grin. "They drove so fast. It was such fun!"

My mother despaired, both at the time and at each retelling. I wonder how she grew up so staid and proper; I wonder how she'd managed to avoid fun and excitement for so long.

The candle flickers; my eyes refocus. I am my mother's mother's mother. At last.

I aimed, once, to be everything she was. But I lost my way.

Born in 1896, she epitomised—to my romantic teenaged mind— all that was Victorian, full of the splendour, glamour, and chivalry of the age. Furthermore, she slunk off at the age of fourteen to be a Suffragette, lying about her age, of course, to be taken seriously (go Granny!). Eagerly chaining herself to railings, brazenly smashing windows, fighting passionately and vehemently for the cause—how could she not be an idol.

One time, so family legend has it, she squared up to a policeman, all five foot two inches of her standing on tiptoes and staring him straight in the eye, neither of them conceding. Just as he looked set to arrest her, she reached up, kissed him on the cheek and skipped away.

Why didn't you let yourself get arrested? asked my grandmother, disenchanted.

Why did you *kiss* him at all? asked my mother in disapproval.

She died when I was fourteen, this woman who had seemed so indestructible; the family felt the loss immeasurably, never stopped feeling it.

On the day of her funeral, the three remaining generations stood side-by-side, hand-in-hand, and celebrated her life. We sat at home, later in the day, and looked through albums of photographs thought long lost. And she was there in front of us again, dressed in finery for a ball; dressed for action and lined up against a wall with fellow Suffragettes with a VOTES FOR WOMEN banner; standing with her family outside their home a year after the outbreak of the Great War, her brother in uniform, ready to join the front line.

We stopped talking when we reached her wedding portrait. She married in the same year as the Queen Mother and looked eerily similar. There was a certain sadness in her eyes; some-what nostalgic for the life she was giving away, perhaps? She loved her husband deeply though, my great-grandfather who I never knew; theirs was a beautiful love story, by all accounts. Because love doesn't have to be stifling; because sometimes it's love itself which can set you free.

My grandmother wept as she turned the pages. My mother gazed at the pictures almost without emotion; it was so hard to fathom what she was thinking with that wry, sad smile on her face. I'd like to think she finally understood her mother and grandmother, but there was disdain and disregard in the way she slammed the pages of the album together and moved the subject on to something else; and I felt sorry that she couldn't love them the way I loved them.

Looking in the mirror now, as the candle flickers and my shadow pirouettes, I am all of these women.

The chemist's bag is suddenly an enemy. Inside the bag are boxes; and inside the boxes there are blister packs of little white tablets, far too many for normal requirements. They wait for me to give up on these women, to give up on myself. Yet it seems too early, when I've not yet kissed a policeman or jumped from a plane.

And so the chemist's bag waits impatiently. I blow out the candle, leaving myself in darkness.

Rain Dancing

She wasn't wearing any shoes. She looked like a ghost, or a perfectly crafted statue moulded into the scenery. Her hair blowing out behind her, her pale face deftly sculpted, unsmiling but full of energy and life. Her eyes radiant, deep and absorbing; eyes that were fixed on me.

But right then she seemed out of reach; almost untouchable.

"Let's go for a walk," she'd said earlier that evening, gazing out of the window. There wasn't much to see: grey buildings, a maze of streets, sullen commuters. But Helen watched with fascination and curiosity.

"It's going to rain," I replied, settling in front of the television, newspaper in hand, sounding more irritable than I'd intended. I flipped channels a few times, stopping here and there something caught my attention briefly, but not for long. "And Die Hard's on later."

"You've seen it a hundred times!"

"And I want to see it again."

"That's your problem," she sulked, sitting down on chair across the room, arms folded, looking for an argument. "You never do anything *different*. You come home from work, sit down and watch telly. You're an old man already!"

"I work hard. When I come home, I just want to relax." The words came out as one long sigh. I was used to this. It was part of an extensive list of grumbles she had against me,

"I only want to go for a walk," she mumbled, as though talking to someone else entirely.

"It's raining!"

Helen wandered out of the room, pouting like a child. I could sense her drifting through the flat; I could hear her banging pots and pans in the kitchen, opening cupboards and letting them slam shut. She switched the radio on and off. She came back and knelt on the floor by my feet, resting her head on my lap, stroking my leg absently until it drove me mad. Her dark eyes, almost black, were wide and teasing.

"Please Gray," she purred, looking up from beneath the fringe that fell across her face. Helen only ever called me Graham when she was angry, really angry, plate-throwing angry. She threw plates quite a lot, and other things; pillows, dirty clothes when I left them lying on the floor. Once, she threw a lamp that I'd given her for her birthday. She looked so beautiful when she was angry.

We walked towards the park, hand in hand, through the rain; I knew I'd have no peace all evening if I didn't. Well, maybe that isn't strictly true: I gave in because I always give in to Helen. I can't resist her. Few people can. I once heard her being described as contagious. She laughed. "You mean, like a disease?" she asked. "No," said the admirer.

She was smiling now, a huge grin that swallowed up her whole face, a triumphant smile. Her hair was stuck to the back of her neck, the rain was dripping from her nose; her face was fresh, youthful. Every so often she stopped and kissed me, long and slow and lingering. My heart beat faster. The scent of her perfume reminded me of holidays; the smell of sizzling summer evenings and frosty winter mornings; everything rolled into one.

Her white T-shirt was transparent by now. Her eyes flashed as I pointed it out, and she pulled her jacket around her, looking up at me out of the corner of her eye with an enigmatic expression. There was something bewitching about the way she was smiling at me; the way women smile when they don't realise the effect they're having.

At the park gate there was a puddle, stretching from one side of the entrance to the other. Helen slipped off her shoes and carried them, one in each hand, swinging them backwards and forwards. She looked back at me before wading through, squealing as the cold water lapped over her feet. She laughed as I tried to jump over and missed. I felt the water seeping into my shoes, squelching into my socks and between my toes.

She tilted her face to the sky, opened her mouth, drank in the water, and wiped the raindrops from her face.

"Come on, I want to go home." I was cold and the rain was dripping from my fringe, running down my face, into the collar of my shirt. I wanted to take her home and lie in her arms until we were both warm again.

She stared at me for a moment, a flicker of frustration in her eyes. Then she suddenly screamed, making me jump, and stared at me with the intensity of a charging bull; her eyes glinting in the orange lamp light. "God! What am I doing with you? You're like my father! You're *worse* than my father! You're so *fucking* boring! You—you…" Her arms flew around wildly. "I'm going to die if I don't get out of this. Do you understand that? You're *killing* me. I feel like I'm suffocating." She stopped and stood very still. Quietly now: "I can't go on like this."

"So, what are you doing with me?" The question physically hurt; a breath-stealing punch. "Find someone else. Find someone who wants to walk in the rain with you. Find someone who…" I stopped, floundering. Helen was wiping a tear from her cheek. She wrapped her arms around me and laid her head on my chest.

"I love you." She pulled away. "I don't want to hurt you." She laughed at the absurdity of her words. "I'm sorry." We faced each other, miles apart, the rain beating against us. It seemed like forever.

"I don't understand what I've done wrong."

She smiled grimly. "Typical male." She wiped away the tears, still flowing, with the back of her hand. "This isn't something new. I've thought about you a lot over the past few weeks. I tried to imagine being with you forever…" Her eyes darted away and back again. "I just… I don't think… don't think we're good for each other… you know?"

I shook my head. "No, I don't know. I love you. I thought…" I stopped as I realised what she was saying. Stopped as the full impact seeped into my head.

"This isn't how I thought it would end."

"It's not an ending." I touched her cheek, feeling the warmth of her skin. "Is it?"

"I'm sorry."

I watched her turn away, her head bowed, her shoulders slumped. She held out her arms and walked along in a completely straight line, one foot directly in front of the other. She was moving slowly, kicking her feet through the puddles. Occasionally she walked backwards slightly, as though she couldn't quite find the strength to leave me standing there alone. She jumped, landing in the middle of a large puddle. Her long white skirt clung to her legs, the shape of them clearly visible, long and slender. She wiggled her toes in the water for a few moments, then walked on.

She didn't look back. I remember that more than anything else. She didn't look back. I wanted to mean more to her than that. I wanted her to turn, because I was sure she'd change her mind. And perhaps she would have, and that's why she didn't.

I could never believe how lucky I was, having someone like Helen in love with me. She was so impulsive, so exciting; she never worried what people thought, she did things, said things, because she wanted to; things that made people stare open-mouthed. She had her pick of a thousand men. But she chose me. I knew she wouldn't stay with me. She said she would, over and over; how she would never leave me, how she loved me so much, too much. But I knew I'd never be enough for her.

She was too far away now, just a shape—a ghost—disappearing, fading into the misty blackness. I saw everything being snatched away from me, every scrap of happiness, every tiny dream…

I chased after her, the urge to hold her was overpowering, the urge to hold *onto* her. She turned around, her eyes big and round, red through tears which she'd no longer been able to control. There was a half-smile on her lips, but she still looked sad.

"Helen…"

She placed her fingers to cover my lips; she reached up and kissed me. She smoothed my hair away from my eyes; she used to do that when she thought I was sleeping. I'd open my eyes and startle her.

I couldn't move. I gazed at her, watching her. She lowered her eyes, allowing them to follow her hands as they wandered up and down my body, stopping at the top button of my shirt. She undid it, then moved to the next, then the next, slipping her fingers inside and running her nails across my chest.

The rain was getting heavier, more constant. I could hear the branches of the oak trees creaking above us, the breeze growing stronger.

Helen took one of my fingers in her mouth and began chewing on it gently. I shivered, fixed to the spot. There were still tears in her eyes. She pulled herself close to me. I could feel the coldness of her body, the dampness of her clothes. I could feel every curve pressing into me, every breath, every heartbeat.

"Do you—do you want to go home?" I shuddered as she nipped at my ear. Every part of my body was aching to be as close to her as possible.

She didn't reply. She took my hand, led me along the path and pushed me down onto the grass. She unbuttoned the rest of my shirt, kissed my chest as she moved herself down my body. I felt her warm lips on my stomach, her hand tugging at my belt.

I heard footsteps; or voices, maybe. I tried to push her away. She laughed. She looked so perfect. Like the purple sunset that enveloped us. She stood up, spinning around and around, her arms spread out, her eyes closed, her face turned upwards, the rain falling on her like a spotlight. Dancing like a ghost.

She fell to the ground beside me, her eyes still closed, her lips slightly apart. I allowed my hands to feel her taut stomach, caressing lightly as though she was a delicate flower, afraid of breaking her. She shivered slightly but shook her head irritably when I asked, again, if she wanted to go home. She pulled away and sat up, hugging her knees to her chest, and resting her chin on them.

"I knew you wouldn't go through with it."

"With what?"

She turned her head away. "Maybe I should just accept you're different. But I wanted to prove to myself that you…" She paused and looked into the distance, as though I wasn't even there. "I guess it really is over." Her voice trembled. She rolled into me, clinging to me.

I tilted her face towards me, kissed her lips, her eyelids, forehead, cheeks, neck. I pushed her T-shirt up, kissed her chest, her breasts, her stomach. She pulled me back up until our lips met, slowly at first, teasing, biting; then more forceful, more frantic.

She straddled me, easing my jeans over my hips, squeezing and manipulating my cock. I laid there, as if in a fantasy, with everything happening around me and having no control. I laid there as Helen enveloped me, rising and falling with a deliberate perpetual rhythm, the moonlight highlighting the side of her face. All the time she was intent on me, her eyes never straying. The rain fell softly down on us; Helen's hair hung in ringlets, with drops of water dangling from the ends. I lay there while everything happened in slow motion.

Her tempo changed. Speeding up, thrusting harder. She threw her head back. Caught her breath. Her hips danced; she leant backwards, gasping. I wanted to touch her, to feel her body straining and tensing, but she held my hands down by my thighs. There was something different; a barrier.

We groaned in explosive unison. Helen stopped, frozen in place. I recall every detail about the way she looked right then, every part of her: her damp skin, her dark hair, her wistful smile, her regretful eyes. She was more beautiful at that moment than she'd ever been.

Then she collapsed forward across my torso, her head buried in my chest so I couldn't see her face. I held her tightly against me, not wanting to let her go, wanting to keep her with me, here and now, forever. As soon as she moved away from me, things would be different. It would never be like this again; I was afraid. I wasn't ready for her to leave. I loved her, and I wanted her.

"You said I wouldn't do it," I challenged her, regretting my tone, my words immediately.

"That doesn't make everything all right. It's just one night."

"And tomorrow will be another night."

She laughed condescendingly, as though I'd just told a terrible joke. "This isn't a game, Gray." She played with the chain around her neck, her fingers running along the inside. "You don't even know what the problem is." She sat up and began to feel around for her clothes. She rolled away, pulled on her T-shirt, pulled down her skirt.

I looked at my watch. Half-past eleven. I should've been in bed at least half an hour ago: I'd never wake up for work in the morning. *What the hell am I thinking?!*

Helen was leaving me. She was sitting next to me right now, thinking about a life without me, perhaps a better life without me. And I was worrying about being late for work?

Maybe I was the wrong man for someone who danced in the rain.

I wanted someone to reach in and drag me out: I didn't know what I was supposed to do next, what Helen wanted me to do. I'd never seen Helen like this before.

I closed my eyes, imagining myself somewhere else, somewhere the sun was shining and the sea was gently lapping at my toes. A different place, a better time. I wanted Helen to be there with me as well, but my mind wouldn't conjure her up. My head was already learning how to cope without her.

"I'm cold," she said, huddling into me. She looked so young, like she needed protecting. Protecting from what? From me. I was the one who was hurting her. I was the one who had to let go. For her; for both of us.

"Do you love me?" she asked.

"More than anything. More than you'll ever know."

Her eyes sparkled. She scrambled to her feet, holding my hands and pulling me up with her. She paused, unsure of her next move; realising, maybe, that this was it, the end. After a while, we simply started walking in silence, back the way we'd come, towards the park gates and the busy main road on the other side.

And we were running. Hand in hand; as fast as we could. Helen screamed with delight. My whole body ached with exertion; my legs stretched out with each stride. We splashed through puddles. We ran until we couldn't run anymore, stopping in the shadow of a large oak tree.

As I leant against the trunk, hunched over catching my breath, Helen started to dance again. Dancing just for me.

Story Credits

Each of these stories has been updated and remastered from their original publications, although still pretty much set in the years they were published. I never feel I am finished writing, and I've loved having the chance to work on my babies again.

That Sadie Thing was published in LIBBON (2006).
Irish Green won third prize in the Writer's Bureau competition (2010).
Beth won first prize in the Ashby Writer's Club (2010).
The Walking Dead was published in Story Cellar Magazine (1996). This version is a complete re-telling of the original story.
Open Windows was runner-up in the Exeter & District Writers Club competition (1997).
Omelette won third prize in the Words with Jam competition (2010).
Shadows of Autumn was commended in the Writers Forum competition (2006).
Portrait of the Painter was runner-up in the Real Writers competition (2000).
The Girl who is Good was commended in The New Writer competition (2008).
Tasting the Grass was published in New Fiction Magazine (1994).
Rain Dancing was published in Raconteur (1994).

Acknowledgements

First, I need to thank the people I thanked in the first edition of this collection. Kyra Lennon, for proofreading and designing the original cover; Linda King, for wise words and opinions in choosing the bonus stories; and Helen Button, for her support from the day I met her, and for being my number one cheerleader.

Thanks to all the editors and judges who read my submissions and competition entries over the years. The feedback and encouragement I was given from the very beginning was a key factor in my continuing to write. And of course, a special mention to the people who thought the stories in this collection were worthy of prizes.

To my family for putting up with my strange ideas, requests, and abruptness when the perfect sentence is on the tip of my tongue and they ask if I want a cuppa.

And thank you to everyone who overlooked the fact that blocking phone numbers is now a common thing and that the title story, written in 1994, would be less likely to happen today.

***

If you enjoyed this collection, please leave a short review on the retailer's website, Goodreads or Bookbub.

Thank you.

About the Author

Annalisa Crawford lives in Cornwall UK, with a good supply of moorland and beaches to keep her inspired. She lives with her husband, two sons, and dog.

Annalisa writes dark contemporary, character-driven stories, with a hint of the paranormal.

She is the author of four short story collections, and her novels Grace & Serenity (July 2020) and Small Forgotten Moments (August 2021) are published by Vine Leaves Press.

For more information visit
www.annalisacrawford.com

Printed in Great Britain
by Amazon

22819716R00067